I0783829

TORN AND *Mended*

E. Ruth Harder

A Russian Hill Press Book
United States • United Kingdom • Australia

Russian Hill Press

The publisher is not responsible for websites (or their content) that are not owned by the publisher.

Copyright © 2023 by E. Ruth Harder

Except as permitted under the U.S. Copyright Act of 1976, no part of this book may be reproduced or transmitted in any form or by any means, electronic or mechanical, including photocopying, recording, or by any information storage and retrieval system, without permission in writing from the copyright owner.

Cover and Book Designer: Coleen Royal
Quotations Source: *Holy Bible, New Revised Standard Version,* Augsburg Fortress, 1990
Library of Congress Control Number: 2023904387
ISBN: 979-8-9879285-2-3

Dedication

I dedicate this novel to the memory of my sister, Alva Jean Welch who suggested I write a book about a leper.

Acknowledgements

Many people helped me in the creation and publication of Torn and Mended.

I am grateful to all who encouraged me to write: my children, grandchildren, sisters and friends, and the Holy Cross Lutheran Church family in Livermore California.

California Writers Club Tri-Valley Writers have given me valuable information and support. George Cramer secured beta readers Gary Lea, and Lani Longshore who handled my manuscript with great care and insight. I am very grateful to them as I could not have done it as well without their input.

I'm indebted to Paula Chinick of Russian Hill Press who provides a valuable service.

Violet Moore, line editor, did a thorough reading with comments and correction of the manuscript. Her knowledge of Biblical history and faith are invaluable to me.

Coleen Royal created my fabulous cover design as well as the book's interior design. She is not only a talented artist, but also my daughter.

To God be the glory because, without his guidance I could not have created this work of Biblical historical fiction.

TORN
AND
Mended

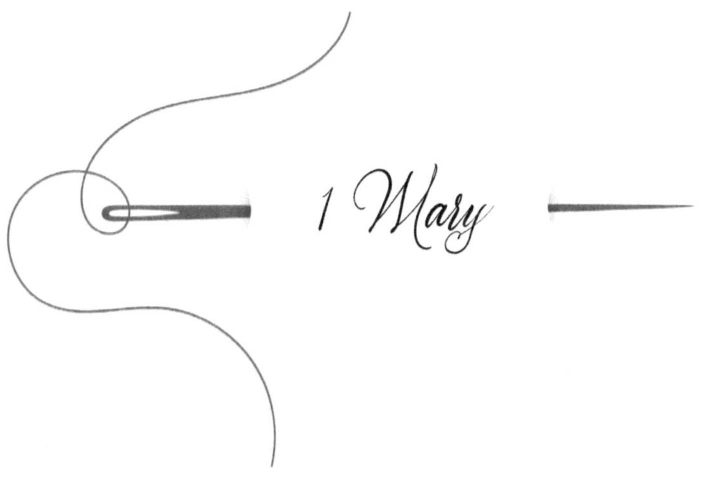

1 Mary

The simple believe everything, but the clever
consider their steps.

Proverbs 14:15

As I carried fresh bread into our house from the outdoor oven, the sun cast my world in bright gold and turned the olive trees into shiny curtains of green and white. My life was a series of sunrises, sameness, and sunsets. My big excitement would be to break off a piece of fresh bread and pop the tasty morsel into my mouth. I came into the kitchen, where my sister Martha bent over a large steaming kettle that hung above the hearth flames.

"Mary, wait for it to cool first," she said. "Did Lazarus leave?"

"I think he and Simon went to Jerusalem some time ago." I tore off a crust of bread.

She made a face at me. "Wonder what is keeping him?"

"Oh, you know our brother. He has not been away very long and is probably with the followers of Jesus. I wish I could be with them."

"Mary, you are getting too old to be trailing after our brother among all those men. What will people say?"

"Maybe I like listening to Jesus?" What I did not say was I loved Jesus. His voice, his beautiful shiny dark hair and beard, his slender brown feet with elegantly formed toes. Everything about him was entirely perfect. I felt elated, like dancing the hora at a festival.

"Hmm." Martha shook her head. She supported the disciples, mostly by serving and providing food. We sometimes mended their clothes.

"Since we are almost out of water and our spring has dried for the season, I could go down to the Gihon Spring." As I waited for her to respond, I said, "Sometimes I want to travel far from Bethany to exotic lands like Simon does." I admired our neighbor, Simon, who traveled and traded many goods in foreign lands. I had listened to him telling my brother of his experiences.

Martha shook her head and frowned at my wanting to go afar. She scooped a spoonful of soup and thrust it in front of me to taste. Pleasant steamy aromas filled the air. She dropped a handful of greens into the kettle. "The Gihon Spring has been there forever. Hezekiah had a tunnel built to bring water from there into the city. YHWH blessed his people with water from the gushing spring in the valley." Martha chopped thyme. While giving me a history lesson, she ignored my offer because she did not want me to go alone, or to go toward Jerusalem at all. She probably feared I would go on and look for Jesus.

"Martha, I already know all about the historical spring. Lazarus is not home, and it will probably be too dark when he gets here. I will go alone for water." I was lighthearted, happy, and secure with my life. With Uncle Elias next door on one side and Simon on the other, we had a good, safe neighborhood.

Damp strands of dark brown hair slipped out of her kerchief and draped across Martha's forehead as she shook her head and shrugged. "Be careful, but you should wait, as you and Lazarus could go tomorrow. You still have some mending to do when you get back if there is enough light."

"Alright. I will hurry." I grabbed two buckets and went out before my sister could change her mind. Uncle Elias had given us wood and leather buckets to make it easier when we needed to go to the spring. I enjoyed a walk for any reason. The air was pungent with the sour-sweet aroma of late plums. My mind was joyful, and I sang to myself as I walked. I trusted YHWH as I had learned from my devout family. I hurried down the Mount Olive Trail toward Siloam's Spring. I was happy to be given a grown-up chore.

The cadence of the running water danced in my ears before I reached the spring. I placed our buckets to catch the flowing water as it cascaded into the pool. Two elderly men sat and waited for a relative to put them into the Siloam pool they believed had curative power. Fresh cool water felt like balm in my mouth as I drank some before the trek up the hill to bring the water home. My arms were unaccustomed to the strain of carrying two full buckets of water. About halfway up, I set them down to rest.

Footsteps of someone climbing echoed behind me. I heard heavy breathing as a man sidled up beside me. His deep voice was friendly. "Where does the trail lead, young woman?"

"To Bethany," I said. I was not accustomed to having a man speak to a woman. The stranger was large, taller than my brother, and had a broad forehead.

"May I carry these for you?" He had an accent, but his words sounded sincere and polite.

"I am alright." Hesitant to trust a stranger, I heaved up my buckets and turned to walk.

"Come on, little woman. You are struggling under the weight of the water buckets. Allow me to help." His voice cajoled, almost fatherly, was very convincing.

My arm muscles strained, but I continued to walk. While I didn't know the man, he had offered. I stopped and looked at him, and he smiled at me behind his dark beard as he grabbed the buckets out of my hands.
It was a relief to be free of the weight. I shook feeling into my numb fingers. "I will show you the way."

"Alright," he said.

I walked fast and assumed the man would follow me, perhaps more slowly since he was burdened with the water. I would offer him fresh bread when I got home. When I turned to tell him about the bread, I looked back and did not see him. My arms prickled an alert.

I wondered if I should go back to find him or hurry home. I walked slowly toward home. In a heat of remorse and anger, I turned and ran back down the trail, but did not see the man who had my water buckets. If I could not find him, we would be out of water. My shoulders sagged, as I feared I would not be allowed to go for water again until I was older.

The sun had left dark shadows as it crept away.

Halfway down, I followed footsteps where someone had trampled dry weeds as they veered off the rocky trail. Among the brush and olive trees, there was a skin tent, and I heard men's voices. I turned back to get Martha or Lazarus if he was home. The man had no business stealing my buckets of water. He could easily have gotten his own. Frustrated and angry, I started to run home.

A large hand clamped my mouth and the man lifted me up with his other arm. He threatened, "Where do you think you are going?"

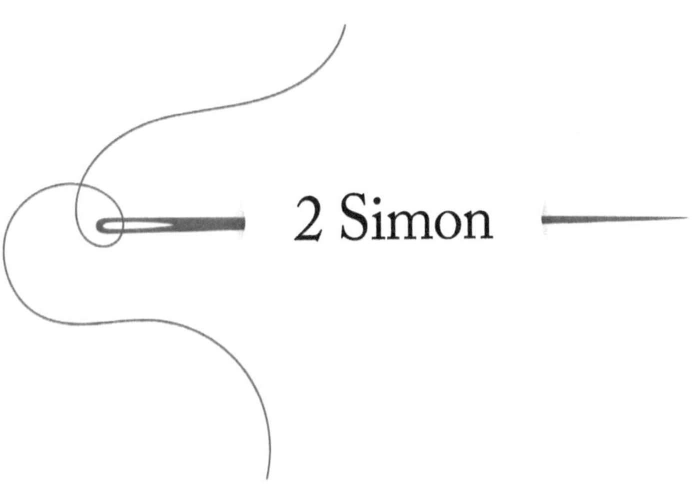

2 Simon

*The human mind plans the way, but the
Lord directs the steps.*

Proverbs 16:9

I had returned to Bethany from business travels to Rome and Egypt and had not gone inside my house, when I saw and greeted my close neighbor, Lazarus. He clapped me on the shoulder. "Simon, we have missed you. So good to have you back. I trust you had a successful journey. Do you have time to sit and visit?" We settled on a stone bench in our mutual courtyard where small birds twittered in shady olive trees announcing the close of the day.

"Yes, to both questions. I hired a crew of stonecutters and artisans to hew out a tomb for a family in Jerusalem. I am eager to hear what has been happening while I was away."

"My friend Jesus from Nazareth has been here preaching in the synagogues and the temple area. He has healed sick people, and he has been standing up to the Pharisees and Sadducees who are questioning him and condemning him and his followers for not obeying their laws."

"Yes, of course, I know Jesus as I saw him a few times at your home. Perhaps he will heal me. I have been afflicted with some insect bites which have crept over my body. Something must have bitten me while I was in Egypt and is causing an awful irritation." I pulled my left sleeve up.

"Oh, oh. I see the lesions on your arm, but are you sure they are insect bites?" Lazarus paused, and his voice was guarded as he said, "It could be much more serious. Of course, I'm not a physician and am not certain, and truly hate to trouble you, but the white sores look like you could have . . . leprosy." He rose from the bench.

"Leprosy?" I sat stricken and in disbelief. Lepers stayed far away from all people, were not allowed to be near anyone, not even their own family, because the disease was evil and could inflict those around them. "Go away from me, dear friend. I do not want you to get leprosy if it is so." I had felt tired and unwell and blamed it on business stress and travel. "Leprosy!" I bowed my head. "Shall I see a physician? I suppose even they do not want to get close to me. Go, my friend, leave me." I could not believe it. The air around me was deadly still. "I will go seek a physician's judgement in Jerusalem."

Martha heard us talking and came outside. "Simon, I am happy to see you have returned." She set a tray of bread, fruit, and tea beside me on the bench. "I have chores to do but wanted to welcome you back."

Lazarus and I enjoyed the bread and tea. When I was sufficiently refreshed, we went down the Mount Olive Trail together.

"Jesus can heal you," Lazarus said.

We went to Jerusalem, did not see a physician, and did not find Jesus.

When we returned home, Martha said, "You need to look for Mary as the day is far spent. She went for water and is not home."

"She dawdles! She probably found a butterfly to follow." Lazarus did not go immediately to find his sister but went toward his door. "I hope it is only insect bites."

Unsure of what to do, I did not go inside my home where my manservant Ott and his wife Naomi waited for me. I left the courtyard, and I sat for a long time beside the Mount Olive Trail. Men whom I had hired were hewing out a new tomb farther over, down below. It was a calm evening and unseasonably warm. I could have wept but did not. Perhaps I was only suffering from bites. After all, I was not yet sure of my leprosy. I longed to hear the sweet lilting voice of Mary, the younger sister of Martha and Lazarus, and wanted to greet her. It felt so odd not to be able to be among people and to see how much the girl had grown.

I wondered how I would stay away from people until this illness disappeared. Is leprosy curable, if indeed it is what I have?

I chuckled to myself. If I was leprous, I could go live among the cavernous tombs with other lepers. While I was there, I could check on the stonecutters and artisans I had contracted to hew the tomb. Would I die there? Would my flesh be eaten by vultures, and my bones left to dry in the wilderness, never to be placed in a proper ossuary inside a tomb?

I kept to the tomb areas and wrapped a cowl over most of my face. People knew I hired men there, so no one need know I had more reason to stay. As I was pacing near where the stonecutters worked, a man stepped out of the shadow of an open cave. He looked miserable, in torn rags. His face was a mass of white sores, and I knew he was one of those who lived in the area among the tombs. He wore a bell and announced weakly, "Unclean."

"Thank you, friend," I said. Staying a short distance away, I bared my arm. "Is this how it begins?"

He nodded his head sadly. "Yes, your white hands and some sores on your face too. It gets much worse. Have you any food?"

I reached into my bag tied about my waist and drew out a round of stale bread. He reached his hand out, then drew it back. "You may need it yourself." His face looked like a mass of small grey pebbles.

"Thank you. I am Simon." I broke the flat round in two and handed him some dry bread. "I am recently returned from business travel. I have not bathed or done ritual cleansing, for obvious reasons."

"Neither have I. Thank you. I am Lemuel." He waited at first, then reached out a gnarled white hand missing his small finger to accept the bread.

Lemuel stepped back into the shadows. I felt little peace in my heart, even though I had made a new friend, kindred only by the disease of leprosy. Indeed, what he had said was true. I wondered where my next meal would come from. I could beg, but people would shun me. The lesions appearing on my face gave away my dire situation. I had paid little attention in the past to idle talk about the disease among people, as I thought it would never apply to me. Some said bathing in the blood of a lamb cured it. I now wondered if it would help me. I was willing to try anything.

I had little food and felt faint. A thought formed. My home was within walking distance. It was dark as I walked slowly to my home in Bethany. It was the place I had prepared to bring my bride, where I had hoped to raise a family. At present, Ott, my manservant, and his family lived there to keep it while I was present or away, and his wife cooked for me. They were not bound slaves, but paid servants. I wondered if I dare come inside and expose them to this dreaded disease.

"At your service, Master," Ott said and bowed low when he answered the door. The lamp in his hand illuminated his ruddy face. "I did not know it was you, as I thought you had again been called away on business."

"Back away from me, because I believe I am unclean and diseased."

Ott gasped and stepped back but remained in the room. "Master, you have been gone longer than usual. How can I be of service to you? I will bring stew, bread and cheese, dates, and wine for you."

"Thank you."

Naomi and her daughter Sara set a table before me and I ate ravenously. The wine soothed my throat but burned my insides at first. I had to speak or might never have the courage to say what needed to be said.

I was betrothed to a lovely young woman named Judith. Our wedding date had been set to occur the next year. Now the unthinkable had happened. I needed to get word to Abner, Judith's father. I could not marry any time soon. I should release her of any obligation. I was sick at heart to think of such a thing because I loved the sight of her and the kind of woman I knew she would be for me. Her father was well known. My despair was almost unbearable. My life had been taken from me. I still lived, but my heart and soul were dashed to pieces as if I had been stoned.

"Since I believe I have leprosy, which you can see with the lamplight on my hands and face, I must tell Judith's parents I cannot marry her. I need to relieve her of the obligation to become my wife. They may keep the partial bride's price I have paid. I trust her father can find another suitable husband for her. Bring me parchment and my writing implements." I was used to writing and keeping track of business matters. When I finished, I carefully rolled and sealed it. I was exhausted and sad as I asked Ott to deliver the message for me. "Wait for a day before delivering it, so no demon from my hand can be laid bare to harm you or Abner." Nothing seemed real. Angry, I was not one to express deep emotions, but inside, I wept.

His voice was sad when he finally spoke to me. "Master, I will deliver the message. Is there anything else I can do for you?"

"I am staying near another leper. It is above the tombs next to the new one my stonecutting craftsmen are hewing. If you would be so kind, I would like delivery of some food twice a week, enough for me and my friend who lives there as well."

"Yes, Master. Will you sleep here tonight?"

I thought for a long while before I answered. I was tempted to say I would stay and come home every night, but I would not endanger him and his family, or any of my neighbors. I shook my head sadly, and when I had finished my sup, I took the provisions and flasks of wine he put in a basket next to the front door, waved to him and his wife across the room, and left.

I slunk away in the dark like a night prowling animal, feeling little better than one of them. A cold sweat chilled my whole being. I had prided myself in being strong, able to handle anyone or anything. My integrity and intelligence had helped me become a thriving businessman. Now I felt weak, and I feared my life would soon end.

I heard the clopping of a donkey and cart wheels on the upper trail which circled Mount Olive, and I wondered who else traveled in the night. It did not matter. Nothing mattered.

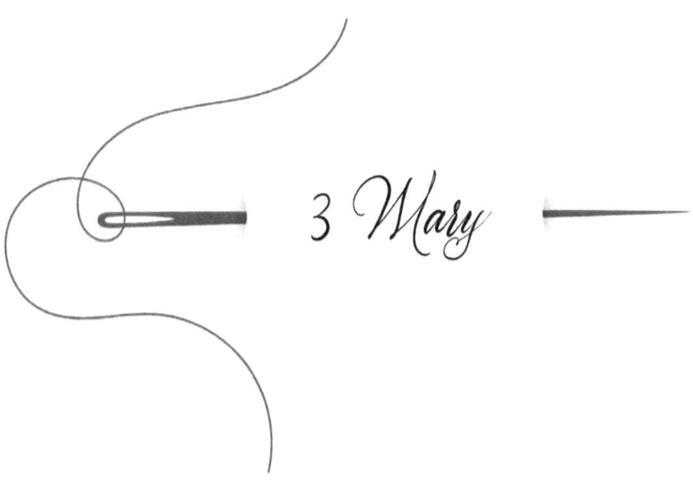

3 Mary

But I trust in you oh Lord; I say, "You are my God." My times are in your hand; deliver me from the hand of my enemies and persecutors.

Psalm 31: 14, 15

Bound hands and feet, I sat cowering in the skin tent as my captor wielded a stick. "What do you want with me?" I asked. "I have no money or anything of value, so let me go." My life pulse threatened to beat out of my chest.

"Hush, woman!"

"Angus, she will be most valuable when we sell her," said the largest man to his companion, the man who had stolen my water.

Sell me? I thought in disbelief.

"It went according to plan. We took the water, and she came back to scold you." They laughed, as their cleverness had worked. I could smell their foul breaths in the air.

I called loudly. "Lazarus!" I wanted Jesus, Lazarus, and my sister to look for me and save me. My breath coursed heavily as if I ran. "You are fortunate I did not bring the authorities with me. Please let me go."

He clamped his big, dirty hand over my mouth. "No, woman. We will take good care of you, as you now belong to us and are valuable to our business."

I was plotting an escape but feared I could not leave without being in more danger. I wanted to prove to myself how clever and grown-up I was, but sadly, I felt like a child amid these large strange men.

They spoke with one another in a language I could not completely understand. I was too afraid to think clearly or scream hatefully at them.

I was alone momentarily in the tent and tried to

roll to the edge and out the opposite side. Once free of the tent, I wondered how I could unbind my hands and feet. I began to bite at the leather thong on my hands, but couldn't loosen it. I rolled out further, hoping to hide under the briars nearby.

"Where do you think you are going, little flower?" The man shook his head. "You will bring a good price for your beauty. I do not want to lose you. My name is Angus." He lifted me as if I were light as a flower.

I was humiliated as I was rudely tossed into a cart that smelled of dust and animal dung. The men covered and secured it, and I became even more fearful, helpless, and angry. Where can they be taking me? The air inside the cart was stuffy as I lay there while we moved by night. I was too frightened to sleep.

In daylight, it became stifling beneath the cover as the sun beat down on it. I tried to move but could not get comfortable. I raised my wrists to my mouth and chewed at the thongs binding me. I tasted salty sweat as I kept gnawing until I felt the leather stretch and loosen a little, and I had thinned one of them. The warmth made it more pliable and after a while, my sore wrists were free. I untied the thongs on my feet but retied my ankles and hands loosely lest the men look. I could be free at a moment's opportunity, but if they glanced in, they could not see I had loosened my thongs. I had hope of getting away as soon as the next nightfall. My life pulse drummed with anticipation.

I drowsed but did not sleep. While the cart covering

was bound and tied securely, there was a small hole in it where I saw it was growing later in the day.

We were not very far up the trail, and they were not going to Bethany or Jerusalem, but around Mount Olive in a brushy area. Below us were some rock-cut tombs.

I could not understand many languages, but I detected Philistine or Canaanite dialects among the men. They are ruthless slave traders. Right now, I needed Jesus to come help me. How I longed for him to appear and work one of his miracles to free me.

I looked around for anything to help enlarge the hole in the covering. The small cart was metal with a rough wood floor and side slats, and I found a long loose splinter. I poked at the hole and tore at the cover slowly, trying unsuccessfully to keep the breach a straight line. If the hole could only be made large enough, I could slip out quietly and roll into the bushes. It was too dangerous to do so during daylight.

I heard footsteps approaching and my life pulse thumped. Someone was untying the cover, so I remained as still as could be. Late sunlight blinded me and air streamed in as the cover was pulled back by half. The man held a flask. "Here, if you are thirsty." He handed it to me, and I made a great show of reminding him my hands were tied.

"Unless you untie my hands, you will have to bring the flask to my lips."

"Oh, alright," he grumbled. "I am Axabal. Remember

who gave you water." I would remember him alright. He smelled putrid of unwashed sweat and rotten breath as he came near enough to tilt the flask of watered wine to my lips for one sip, but now I was thirstier than ever. I wanted to yell out but did not.

The cart moved onward, but I didn't know where they were taking me. It began to get shadier and cooler, so I determined we had reached the grove on the far side of the mount. I felt as if I would die of thirst. I could endure it no longer and called out, "Angus, why are you starving me when I am so valuable? I am near death from hunger and thirst." I heard the men talking among themselves, and it sounded like an argument ensued.

Angus, who had stolen my buckets of water, lifted the cover. "Did you speak, my little flower?"

"I am thirsty as he only gave me a small sip," I rasped and coughed.

He watched me for what seemed like a long time, then reached down with a strong arm to sit me upright part way. He put the flask to my lips, pouring water all over me as he tipped it. "Very well," he said.

As the cart rolled along I was lulled to sleep. Groggy, I thought I heard my brother whisper, "Are you alright, Mary?"

"Help me." Sadly, it was a dream.

We stopped somewhere, and they had not fed me or let me leave the cart to relieve myself. My skin prickled in spite of my resolve to be brave.

"Angus, please, can you let me come out of the cart to relieve myself?"

The men had been murmuring among themselves and stopped when I spoke. They chuckled. Silence prevailed except for a night bird call. I waited a little and called again, "I really need to go relieve myself. You may even watch if you choose." My life pulse sounded like a drumbeat in my ears.

They laughed and talked to each other, rumbling. Footsteps approached as the cart halted. Angus peered inside. "Come, my little flower, and I will help you up." I wriggled around and finally sat up. He grabbed me roughly but deposited me on my feet lightly. He reached down and untied my feet and hands not commenting about the loose binding. "Do not try to run," he said.

"Thank you," I said, trembling. My feet had no feeling, then came alive with prickles.

"Come this way." He put his arm around my back and guided me into the brush. "It is dark, and I cannot see you, so do what you need to do."

I thought to engage him in conversation, and the first thing I could think of came out of my mouth. "Have you ever met a man named Jesus?"

He chuckled. "A few, yes. Which one did you have in mind?"

"He has a group of men following him everywhere he goes, and he has healed at least one person, probably more."

"A healer, no, I don't know him."

I didn't pursue the conversation. I crept slowly into the thick brush and looked up at the sky to get my bearings from it. I breathed a quick prayer. The last glow of the sunset was not visible; it must be late. I was tempted to keep going away to try to find help, but I knew the large men would overtake me. I took my time, as it felt wonderful to be upright. My legs and feet stung as if I stepped on a sharp rock as feeling came back to them.

"You will not try to leave, my little flower."

"No, I am here," I answered. "It feels so good not to be cramped and suffocating in the cart. I am thirsty and hungry."

He led me to a cushion of soft ground, and said, "Sit down."

I sat, thankful it wasn't a briar patch or hard rocks. Nearby their donkey was bedded down for the night. Angus touched my shoulder firmly and left, saying, "Stay there." I heard the whirring and clacking of night insects and felt the cool breeze gently soothing my sore body with its balm. Any other time, I would have felt at peace. I wanted to flee, but knew it would be futile.

He came back with water in a leather flask, some bread, and a piece of cheese. He put the flask to my mouth, and my unbound hands quickly held onto it to keep it from spilling. When I had finished most of the water, he set it down and put a morsel of bread and cheese in my palm. I chewed slowly. It was not much, but enough to appease my hunger. "Where are we going?"

"Ah, it is a secret I must keep from you, but sometime you will be on a boat, traveling across the sea," he said. "I would ask to keep you for myself, but I have not the money or the place to have you as my woman." He licked his lips as if he were enjoying the flavor of a tasty morsel.

He helped me up, walked me to the cart, and lifted me to put me inside. He closed the flap of the cover but did not tie it.

After a long while, the low murmur of voices stopped outside. I raised to partial sitting and inched the cover ever so slowly, not making a sound. I peered out at the starry sky, where the moon was only a small arc of light. The air was fresh and I let it flow over me, to refresh my body a little, but it did not refresh my spirit.

Angus had not retied my feet and hands. I breathed easier as I inched out of the cart, but I caught my foot on the edge, fell, and landed on the hard earth with a thud. I started to get up and run. Angus hurried to me and asked, "Are you hurt?"

"No, I was trying to come out as the water I drank caused an urgency and I did not want to disturb your sleep."

"Little flower, I will take you to the place again." He sounded gruff, and rubbed his eyes. "Do not run."

I tried to think of what to do next. There was nothing, except go and relieve myself again "It is so dark," I said. "I am glad you are here to help me." I wanted him to think I needed his protection.

He bound my hands when I returned. "Get in there

and go back to sleep," he admonished. "I need to rest, too, and tomorrow will be a long day." He gave my lower back a firm pat as I fell into the cart. I felt humiliated, but not defeated.

I waited again for what seemed like an eternity. I reached over to the place where I had enlarged the hole in the cover. It was only large enough for a hand. I used my secured hands, afraid to undo them even though they were loosely tied. Small rips by small rips, and I looked at the opening. It was not yet big enough for me. I listened. I thought someone was approaching the cart, and I held my breath.

My life pulse drummed and my breath came in heaving starts as I tried to control my fear. Something besides the cart smelled foul to me, and I realized it was my own breath. He had not retied my feet. I wondered how long it would be before my brother or Jesus would come. Did they think I had run away or was dawdling for a very long time? I must keep my faith in Jesus, as I was sure he would help me. He and Lazarus would show up. Simon was home again, and he had influence in Jerusalem. He could get authorities to come looking for me.

I slept fitfully and awakened to hear the hitching of the donkey. Soon, we were moving on the trail. I despaired. While I knew my family had no idea of what had happened to me or where to look, I wanted them to find me. I wondered how Jesus, who seemed to know everything and worked miracles, had abandoned me. My faith waned.

4 Simon

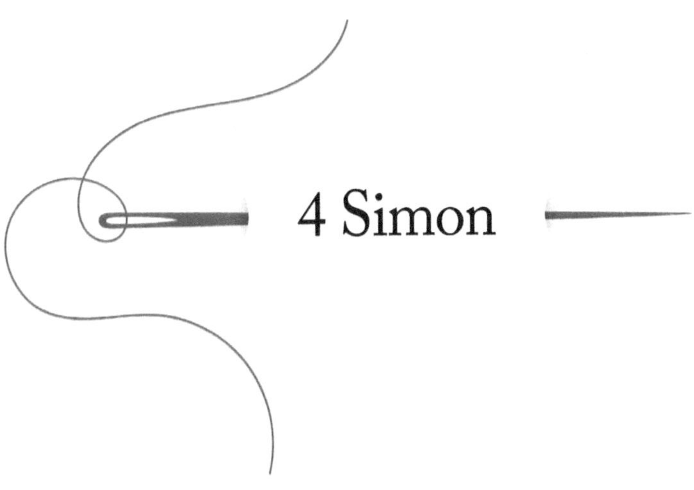

My days are past, my plans are broken off, the desires of my heart. They make night into day; "The light, they say, is near to the darkness."

Job 17:11, 12

I crept around near tombs and hoped no one would see me. It probably did not matter if one of my friends saw me, but I wanted the craftsmen to think of me as the healthy man who had contracted them to work. I sometimes watched the foreman of the stonecutters from my vantage point, hidden by a stone that would one day be formed to close up the cavern. My food lasted a few days as I had little appetite. I looked for Lemuel as I wanted to befriend him, share food, and talk. I like talking with people and missed him, and hoped he was alive.

One day I heard the faint tinkling of a bell. "Lemuel," I called. "I am up here by this gnarled old tree."

Quietly, except for the bell, he made his way up to me. He nodded and sat. It was a comfort to have him beneath the tree with me. I suppose it was enough he had another human near him. He looked dustier and more disheveled than the last time I had seen him. I did not ask where he had been. He sighed as one relieved to sit and rest.

"Lemuel, I have some food for you." I handed him a chunk of bread and a piece of cheese. He took it and ate hungrily. "My manservant will bring us more food and leave it next to the place where the men are working. He comes late in the evening when they have gone home. I told him to bring enough for two people, and he does twice a week."

Lemuel cleared his throat, and I realized he must

be parched. I handed him a skin of wine. Ott would bring more tonight.

"Do you have a family?" I asked.

"I did once. I had a father and mother, brothers, and a sister. My parents died, my sister married, and I have one brother left. I do not see him, as I do not want him to suffer with this illness. I was married, but I have not seen my wife and children since I got leprosy. I asked my brother to take her as his wife and care for her and my children as if I was dead. Do not judge me, as it is almost true since I have no life." He sighed deeply.

I was honored Lemuel had bared his soul to me. "Have you tried any cures?"

He snorted and chuckled softly. "The blood of a dog is supposed to cure if you drink it. It did not. Washing in the blood of a lamb or goat did not help. I had to do these things during a full moon, and never on the Sabbath. I adhered to all the stipulations. Nothing, as you can see, has helped me. Short of a miracle, we are both condemned with this disease."

"How long have you had leprosy?"

"For a few years, but I have lost track of time. One miserable day leads to the next, and it is always the same as the one before. Some days are worse, as even when people see me from afar, they run the other way, and some yell at me or throw stones to make me go away. It is why I stay among tombs where few people come."

"How sad for us. Are there more lepers near us? I have not seen any except you."

"There are others. Many are shy, remain hidden, or simply sit beside the road begging. All have little hope. Few people help us. I have a leper friend named Unabel, who used to come up here where you and I sit. I heard his bell a few days ago and followed the sound a short way then lost him. He is gravely ill. Would you come with me to look for him?" His voice was tentative and sad.

"I have little else to do." We walked in the area above the tombs for some time. He lay in the shadows, his clothing caked dark grey, the same as the earth. He was not moving, and I feared I was seeing my own fate. Lemuel bent down to Unabel and nodded to me. "He feels no more sadness and despair."

"Has he any family to bury him?"

"No one who will claim his body. We must go into the dirt area where we see no large trees or rocks and dig a place for his bones. It would be terrible to allow wild animals to pick at his flesh. Worms may already be at work."

We wanted to dig a shallow grave as best we could in the wilderness of many rocks. I did not have a shovel to dig with, and thought of going to get Ott, but Lemuel found two sharp, flat stones. We began to move rock and earth. My hands chafed and bled, but I did not care. I had started to lose feeling in them anyway. Lemuel and I both labored diligently, but it took us the better part of the day. After sweating a lot, we had made a hole in the earth large enough for the small man's remains. "No one would have bothered, but he had become like a brother to me," Lemuel said. "I am glad you are here with me to help."

I had no spices to anoint his body. We wrapped him in the ragged robe he wore. I found it difficult to look at what was left of the man's face. A grey lump where his nose would have been and his eye sockets—one a grainy black blister and the other, a marbled shiny stare. I tore a sleeve from my robe and wrapped his head. He had only stumps for feet as the disease had taken its toll, so he had not felt when thorns pierced or rocks severed his toes. I felt ill thinking about what he had endured.

"It was what we needed to do. May his soul rest with YHWH or Elohim." We each bowed respectfully, but no prayers were said as we did not know which deity he worshipped, if any, or what he would have preferred. I put a plain stone next to Unabel's grave to mark it, but we did not know who his relatives were or how to contact them. We were already unclean, so touching a body did not seem to warrant purification as it normally would have in our tradition. We were his only family, and I wondered if we should sit shiva for seven days. I smiled sadly.

We walked back in silence at first. Lemuel was limping, and I tried not to notice he wore rags on his feet instead of sandals. The awful consequences of our situation gave me a wrenching feeling in my breast. I looked at my friend sadly. "If you die and I find your body, rest assured I will bury you as we did your friend. No family will ever touch one as unclean as we are."

"If you die, I will do the same for you, Simon."

And so, my life's final plan was set for my burial, unless Lemuel died first. I would have no one to take care of my final resting place. I watched the men down below who had made a large dent in the earth, hewing deeper into the stone so they were inside and out of my sight. I did not need to be near the excellent craftsmen, and the foreman would pay them their wages I had given him to administer. After all was completed, I would need to finalize the payment the man had given me to dig his family's burial place.

The next day, a disturbance echoed from the cavern below. Voices rumbled like a storm. I had almost dozed off, so it startled me more than it should have. "Is anyone hurt?" I stood and yelled, thinking I needed to intervene. Then I realized I could not help anyone, and neither could Lemuel.

A man was carried out by two fellow stonecutters. I could see his head was bleeding. They laid him at the opening and went back to work. I was in a dilemma, as I could not risk going down or seeking help. I looked as close as I dared and was satisfied it was not my foreman. He would be seeing to the man's care. Ordinarily, I might have been called to set things straight. Perhaps the injured man would lie there and die. I did not want it on my conscience, so I did the unthinkable.

I told Lemuel I was going up toward my house, and he should stay and watch so he could tell me if anything happened while I was gone. Lemuel nodded his head and remained seated.

I crept toward my home even though it was daylight. I hoped to somehow get the attention of Ott. He could then obtain help for the injured worker. I grabbed some small pebbles on my way and kept to the sparse shrubbery beside the trail as I walked in case someone should meet me.

When I arrived near my home, I looked at the windows, which were up high, and hoped I could throw some pebbles there without ruining anything. I aimed carefully, and tossed small stones at my own window. I was amused at myself for performing a child's prank.

I heard no sound, so I thought Ott was out buying provisions or with his wife and children at her parent's house. I tried again, and the pebbles hit their mark. Suddenly my front door was flung open. "Who are you boys, and why are you pelting me with small stones?" Ott yelled.

"Over here. It is Simon. I do not want to come near to you, but I need your help. A stonecutter down below has a head injury and the men have put him out on the porch of the cave they are digging, and left him alone. Would you be so kind as to take a look and send for help for him? I will pay you extra."

"Shall I do it now?"

"Please. There may not be much time. I am keeping my distance up above by the gnarled tree, but I can hear when you get there. I am hurrying away now."

I had settled next to Lemuel and was awaiting the appearance of Ott below when the foreman, Samabel, came out and inspected the wound on the man's head. He poured oil or something on the injury. He spoke to the man in a language I was casually familiar with.

The injured dark-skinned man opened his eyes, and I breathed a sigh of relief. At least he was not dead. The foreman went back inside. In a short while, Ott came near the man on the porch. He had some cloths and dressed the wound, speaking kindly to the injured man and asking him if he was hurt elsewhere. The man touched his hand only to his head, and said, "Samabel came and looked at the wound."

Ott came part of the way up to where I sat. "I think it is only a head injury," he said. "His foreman was there before me, but I did not speak with him. I am leaving your basket of food right here instead of down there. Is there anything else I can do for you, Master?"

"I trust you have not heard back from Judith's father."

"No. I gave the parchment to his manservant and left."

I was sick at heart as well as in my ravaged body. The only good things were I had a friend, a trusted manservant, and the tomb stonecutting was going according to plan.

What else would I lose besides my freedom to

marry and have friends other than fellow lepers? I thought about the story of a man named Job, possibly a true tale my father had shared with me while I was a young boy. I could now relate to Job's suffering in many ways. My faith in God was not strong. Lately, I had often wanted to curse YHWH. Where was the Lord to allow such misery? And I kept asking, "Why me?" A coldness crept into my soul. I reached for a flask of wine and took a long swallow.

5 Mary

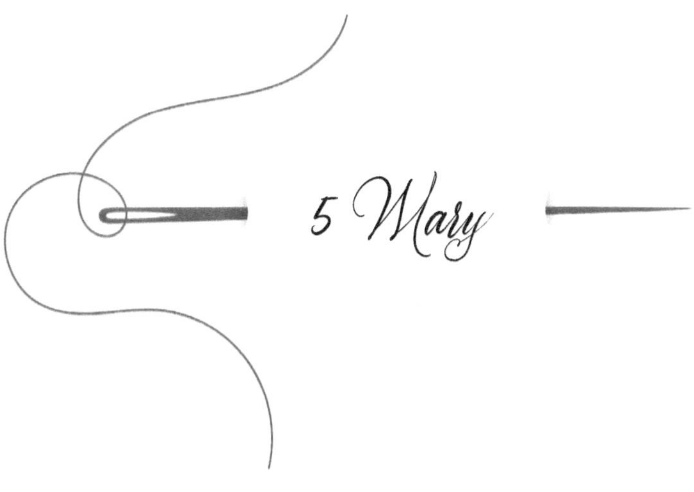

Vindicate me, O God, and defend my cause against an ungodly people; from those who are deceitful and unjust deliver me!

Psalm 43:1

I tried to stop being fearful and angry, as it did not help me find a way to escape. With nothing to do inside the miserable cart, I decided to use pleasant memories to calm myself. I recalled one day when the rays of sunlight were peering over the rise of green and brown hillsides in the distance, and overhead the moon was a pale white orb reluctant to take its leave. No breeze played in the small shrubbery beside the road as I hurried along, trying to catch up with Lazarus and his friends. The villagers in Bethany were busy with sweeping and other morning chores. Some called out greetings. The men were going down the Mount Olive trail, then the road up to Jerusalem. I knew I shouldn't follow my brother, but I loved hearing Jesus and his friends talking about all manner of things.

"Mary," I heard my sister Martha call after me from our home. I should probably answer, but I didn't want to. She would insist I come and help her with household chores. She did not have an interest in the young men. Martha had been betrothed and her intended husband had died, leaving her the home where we now lived. She dedicated her time to serving Jesus and his followers.

I heard a bird twitter, and I went off the path into the bushes and vines beside the road. I fell to the earth in what sounded to me like a great noise as I landed, tangled in the vines. My hands tingled and burned, and my breast heaved as I breathed. I shook my head in disbelief, but gradually regained my balance and stood. I was glad no one was close enough to see me.

I heard low voices as Jesus and his group of disciples stopped around the next bend. I kept out of sight behind a small bush, as I knew Lazarus would send me home. I was especially fond of Jesus. His voice was calming and melodic like singing. I clung to his words, trying to soak them up like a cloth absorbs water.

"Believe in God, believe also in me," Jesus said.

"I believe in you," I whispered.

"Come out little Mary. Why are you hiding?" His voice was sweet like honey.

How did Jesus know I was behind the bush? I stood and timidly walked toward the group. My brother Lazarus frowned. His friend had spoken.

"Where are you going on this fine day?" Jesus asked.

"For a breath of fresh air," I said, not entirely true.

"We are walking the fifteen furlongs to Jerusalem, so I suggest you return home. Martha will be worried." Lazarus sounded kind but looked at me sternly in his protective older brother way.

I turned about slowly, hoping Jesus would ask me to stay. Jesus paid attention to his friends who had questions. I gave up and wandered back to the house where I knew Martha would scold me for going away without telling her.

I had so many questions rolling around in my mind about life, mostly mine. Would I be living with my sister and brother the rest of my life? Would someone like Jesus, who was the son of a craftsman, be a good husband for me? I could love a man like him. He was a kind, gentle, average-height man and certainly looked nice with his shining long Nazarene hair and beard. He had recently helped Lazarus repair our table and bench. He was a good craftsman and ever so patient. I had heard about how he took small children in his arms and blessed them, so I was sure he would be a good father. I daydreamed as the white arc of the moon disappeared and the sunlight streamed fully upon the earth around me.

"Mary, where have you been?" Martha stood in the doorway with her hands on her hips. "How have you already gotten your clothes dirty?"

Back to reality, how I would love to hear my sister's voice, even scolding. But I was a captive, cramped inside a cart going somewhere unknown. Would I die in slavery? My heart ached.

My reverie was broken abruptly by a girl's plaintive cry.

I had sensed us traveling downhill, and then over more rocky terrain. We were among stones, perhaps off the trail. Her scream pierced the air. Sheep bleated. She yelled, "Stop! No, please let me go. I need to tend these few sheep who have little to eat. I have no money or goods for you to steal." There was a scuffle, and men talked loudly among themselves. Someone pulled back the cart cover, and a young woman was dropped in on top of me. Her knees were like stones as they dug into my legs.

Her bloody hands were tied behind her and her

ankles bound. "No, no," she moaned. She closed her eyes as if to shut everything out. She was my age, or near it, and I was sorry she had been seized.

"I have been in this cart for a long time, more than three days and nights, I think. With three men, it is impossible to get free of them. My name is Mary. What is yours? Can you understand my Aramaic?"

"Carabel. Yes, my mother was a half-Canaanite, and I speak Aramaic, some Hebrew, and a few other dialects from my father, who is a Judean. We are herders, doing the best we can among the rocky soil where there is little grass for the sheep. I have to move them around until I find suitable grazing. My parents' small home is over the other hill from here." She began to sob.

I said, "I am an orphan as my parents both died three years ago when I was ten, my sister Martha fifteen, and brother Lazarus eighteen. These men want to sell us as slaves. I thought one of them, Angus, was nice, but he wants to make money like the others. His kindness stopped after I tried to get away."

Carabel kept crying bitter tears. She rolled off me to crowd into the bed of the cart. "I used to have a dog who helped me with the sheep, but he disappeared. I think he was probably eaten by a wild animal. I called him Woolfy, and I always felt protected from harm when he helped me herd the sheep. If he was still with me, the men would have been attacked and bitten before they could have gotten near me."

"You have had a different life than mine. I never had a dog or a herd of sheep to handle."

Carabel stopped crying and sniffed her nose. We lay cramped side by side, knees bent, in companionable silence as the cart rolled on to wherever they were taking us. I asked, "Have you heard about a man named Jesus?"

"No, I don't think so. Why do you ask?"

"He is a good man, a teacher who has a cluster of young men and a few women who follow him around as he teaches. He has healed people. At a wedding in Cana, he changed stone jars of purification water into wine when the host ran out of wine for his guests. He is an amazing man, and some say he is divine."

"Yes, amazing, and unbelievable. I do not know much about him, but your voice tone sounds as if you are enchanted."

"I am in awe of him and respect him," I said. I was glad the cart was not light enough for her to see the warm color I felt creep into my face.

"You love him," Carabel said. "I have never found anyone to love except my mother who is ill and dying and my dog who disappeared."

"I am sorry," I murmured, not sure how to respond.

I lost track of time but amused myself thinking of Jesus and how his voice was so soothing to me. I remembered how he had said, "I am the good shepherd." I hoped he would come and free me and my shepherdess friend from our captors.

Caught in our discomfort together, we said very little to each other. The men gave us bits of bread and some water to keep us alive but did not let us get out to relieve ourselves. We reeked of sweat and all our bodily excrement odors. The buzzing of flies or other insects hovered around our cart. I was miserable and thought the trip would never end. I was fearful we could die in the cart before we came to their destination. There was no feeling in my feet and hands.

One day, the cover was removed and the light blinded and hurt my eyes. Two big women looked in on us. They spoke in a language I could not understand. Carabel knew what they were saying, and talked with them. She turned to me and said, "These two have been ordered to take us to the baths and put fresh clothing on us." A wind blew over us, rustling the loose cart cover.

"I do want to be clean," I said. I thought, I can outrun them if my ankles are freed. They will have to unloose our feet so we can walk. Axabel came and lifted Carabel out of the cart, then secured the cover again with me inside. It was very warm, and I smelled the stench of rotting fish and sea air, and all the odors turned my stomach. The hole in the cover was only wide enough so I could see a little of our surroundings. We were at a seaport, but I didn't know where. I loosened my wrist ties which they had not noticed weren't secure. I eased to a sitting position and worked at the thongs binding my ankles. They were raw and chafed from being tied for so many hours. I wiggled my numb feet and toes to get the feeling back. Surely the women would come for me any moment, so I lay down in my own filth, with the thongs loosened around my ankles. I wasn't sure of my plan, but I wanted to be as free to run as possible.

One woman came back without Carabel, and I wondered what had happened to her. She was not put back in the cart. When the woman lifted me out, she grabbed my ties, pulled them off, and tossed them inside the cart. I was walked to a bath, where stone steps led down to the water like a mikveh, only it was larger. One woman wrapped in a cloth was leaving the bath. No one else was there. It smelled musty, but the water looked clear. I wanted to feel clean again. The woman spoke to me in broken Aramaic. She asked me to remove my garments, which I gladly did as they were soiled and stank. When I stepped into the cool water, my feet felt as if I had stepped on thorns with bare feet. Once in the water, I wanted to remain and enjoy it, but the woman made gestures with talk to encourage me to wash my body with a perfumed rag. I washed as slowly as possible. Her large hand reached out and her round face looked pleasant when she bade me leave the bath. She motioned for me to sit on the side of the pool. I remained there naked, drying naturally with no towel. In a short while she reached down and pulled me up, and I realized she was very strong. I felt weak. She was probably not a woman, but a eunuch.

I was taken to a room where there was all manner

of clothing. The person gestured to an outer robe made of yellow cotton and embellished with curling green fronds and pale pink flower embroidery. An under tunic of natural fabric was given to me, and I put it on and then the robe. It felt so good to be clean and refreshed. I reached up to touch my hair and it felt wet and clean. I combed it and tried to untangle it with my fingers.

Outside in the sunlight, I saw Angus, who looked away from me. Axabel held Carabel by the hand and was speaking with her. She was clean and freshly dressed in a tan and green robe, but she looked fearful. The other slaver was speaking with a sea captain. The eunuch still had my hand in a tight grip, lest I get the idea to run. I longed for Jesus, Lazarus, Martha, Simon, or any of the followers. If only a familiar face appeared I would not feel so frightened and alone. I was trapped, even though I had my bindings off, was clean, and no longer stuffed inside the miserable cart. I wondered desperately what would happen to Carabel and me. She was pretty in a flat-faced, sloe-eyed way, with wavy dark amber hair swept to one side beneath a tan scarf. We exchanged anxious glances, wondering what was next, but we did not speak. I had a sinking feeling inside, sick to my stomach, and very afraid of what would happen to me.

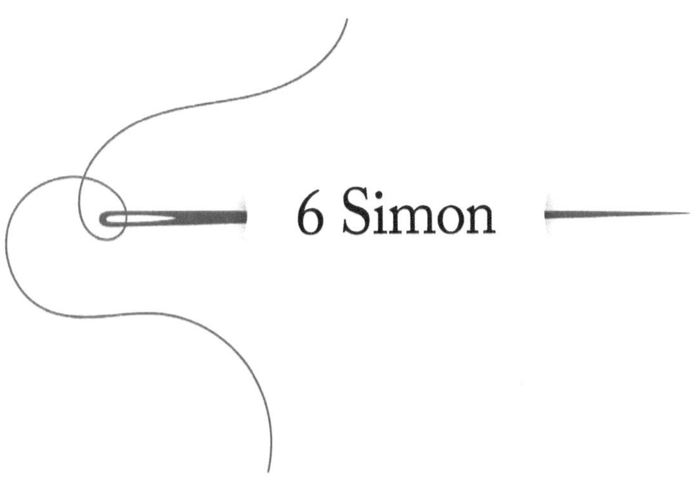

6 Simon

My god, my God, why have you forsaken me? Why are you so far from helping me; from the words of my groaning?

Psalm 22:1

My tears stung my eyes and I could not feel them on my face, but the sores on my neck burned on one side. I hated myself. I hated everyone and everything. Strong burning liquid belched up in my throat and tasted bitter. I knew I smelled bad and I, who had always been particular about cleanliness and bathed regularly, did not care. Lemuel had gone off somewhere. I remembered Lemuel had no sandals and reminded myself to bring an extra pair if I went back to my house.

I rolled in the dust to bring some relief to my sore body, but it did not help. If I went home, bathed, and took a ritual cleanse in my mikveh, would it make me any more comfortable? I would not endanger Ott and his family. I ate little but drank both flasks of wine. As I tilted the second one to my lips, I was surprised to find it empty. I wondered if the spring on Mount Olive had dried this season. Would rains come soon? "Not soon enough YHWH!" I shook my fist at the heavens. My parents had taught me not to ever express anger at our creator YHWH, but I was sorely vexed right now.

I wondered what demon had infected me with the dread disease I now tried to keep from giving others. Ott had brought me a small bell in one of the baskets of food. I wore it now. No one would recognize me, as I was unkempt, with my arms mere bones with sore skin drawn over them. I was certain word had gotten around about my affliction, especially after I had renounced my espousal to Judith. Lemuel and I shared many moments of bitter discussion and quiet desperation.

Lemuel appeared silently and sat beside me. I said, "Perhaps it is time for us to go into Jerusalem and sit by the road to beg. If I cannot work, I will have to let my manservant go. Hopefully, I can keep my home, but I do not want to defile it with my evil leprosy, so I cannot even stay there."

He stood. We walked slowly down Mount Olive and back up toward Jerusalem, two men who despised themselves, hated their lives, hated everyone who could live without restrictions. Side by side, we strolled the streets with our little bells tinkling, and our voices raised plaintively, "Unclean. Unclean."

People avoided us and hurried out of our way to the opposite side of the street. A Roman guard, with his gladius at the ready, came near and then backed away when he saw our situation. He yelled, "You dogs, go away from here. Your evil bodies will infect the whole city. Leave, or I will pierce you with my long sword."

"Pierce me if you dare. It would be a kindness," I said, my voice raspy with mockery. I laughed derisively and lunged toward him. Lemuel nodded and smirked.

As the guard gave me a look of horror, still brandishing his gladius, he backed away, leaving us. Later I recalled the satisfaction it had given me as the only positive incident of the day.

Not so when I saw Abner, Judith's father. I felt ashamed, worse, seeing him as my hopes had been dashed regarding our formal betrothal rites. He had most of the bride's price I had promised and agreed upon. Very little had been left to do except formality, but of course, none of it would happen. Had he recognized me? Was he even expecting to see me begging on the streets? I did not speak to him but watched him pass on the other side of the road as all of the passersby were doing. He turned back briefly, dug into his waist pouch, and threw coins toward where Lemuel and I sat. We both scrambled in the dust and stones in the street for a few leptons.

"You may have all the coins," I said.

"No, no." Lemuel held gritty leptons out to me, but I would not take them. I did not know where either of us could spend them.

A man who was walking on the other side of the street yelled, "Go away, you unclean dogs. Go back to the tombs where you belong."

Two tousle-haired boys grabbed pebbles from the street and flung them at us, laughing and shrieking, "Go away!"

We stood. It was no use. We nodded to each other and walked away, avoiding people, our little bells tinkling. "Unclean, unclean."

"I have had more than my fill of the good people and life in Jerusalem," I scoffed. Lemuel nodded sadly. My sorrow was as if I had lost someone dear to me, and I ripped my sleeve. The person was me.

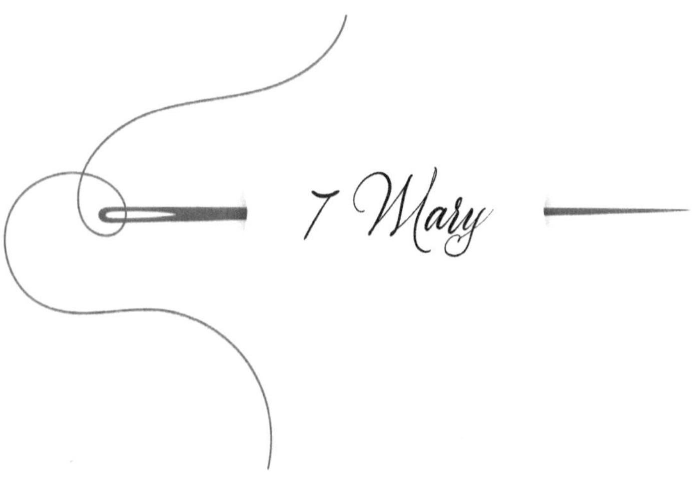

7 Mary

You cast me into the deep, into the heart of the seas, and the
flood surrounded me, all your waves and your
billows passed over me.

Jonah 2:2

Men called to each other as they loaded cargo onto a ship. Some men in a fishing boat were arguing about where to fish. The dark-haired captain of a ship in port nodded to me, then went about business with some man dressed in a grey robe. Where am I? Mostly I was glad to be out of the cramped, smelly cart. It was oh so wonderful to have my aching body soothed and at last be clean.

After our cleansing and dressing in fresh clothes, Angus came and gave the eunuchs some money. I looked around for a convenient way to escape as Angus was momentarily distracted. I started walking away from the boat loading area and ducked behind a large man. When he moved, I did and hoped I could not be seen. The man turned around abruptly and left me standing in the open as if nothing had happened. I would have to try again, but not now.

Angus smiled and put his arm firmly around my shoulders. The eunuchs strolled off. Carabel was escorted by Axabel, and we were loaded like fragile cargo onto a sailing vessel in the port. We each were given a small sack that held some clothing. My knees wobbled as I walked up the plank onto a ship. The sea captain with whom the other man had been speaking greeted us in Aramaic as we came aboard. "Hello, women. You will be seen to your room."

Angus came aboard, but not Axabel or the other slaver who had brought us in the awful cart. I looked longingly at the shore as we set sail. "Where do you suppose we are going?" I asked Carabel.

"Axabel said we might be going to Egypt, or maybe an island nation somewhere across the Great Sea."

I felt like crying but thought I should remain quiet and observant. Perhaps I could find out more if I were to listen as men spoke to each other. Angus grabbed both of us around our waists and almost carried us down some steps to a little room. In it, there were two multicolored blankets and two grey cushions. "Stay here," he said.

I plopped on one cushion. Our darkened room smelled like fish and mold. Angus left the room without a word to either of us. I wondered where we were to relieve ourselves, and whether they would provide us with food and water. Carabel sat cross-legged on the other cushion. "Axabel told me we would be fed and cared for aboard this boat. I am very hungry, are you?"

"I'm thirsty and a little hungry. Perhaps they will bring us some food. Since we are valuable, I am sure they do not intend to starve us."

I sat with my eyes adjusting to the darkness of our small room, and I soon spotted something in one corner. "There is a jar when we need to relieve ourselves," I said. "No need to walk far."

"Good. I am glad to be clean and out of the awful cart, but I long to find some way to free ourselves. They did not secure our hands and feet this time."

"Unless you swim, freedom is not likely." I was gloomy.

"I can swim. We used to live by a stream, and I would go in and paddle around while my father fished.

I wish we had never moved to the hill country outside Jerusalem. My father thought we would have a better life, and my mother wanted to be nearer her people," Carabel said.

"Alas, I cannot swim, but now I wish I had been able to learn."

Angus came into our tiny room carrying flatbread, dates, goat cheese, and a flask. "Feed yourselves and enjoy the wine." He looked at me with an expression I could not discern in the darkness. "My little flower, are you comfortable here? Is there anything else I can do for you?"

"Better here than cramped in the awful cart! Now let me go free," I said. My body ached.

"The sea would swallow you if I let you go right now." He shook his head, turned, and left us.

I ate slowly as there was nothing else to do. Carabel grabbed bread and cheese hungrily. The flask had watered wine in it, and its contents eased the tension in my shoulders as it infused my body. "Have some more." I offered it to Carabel. She sipped again and smiled at me. She and I slowly nibbled our food, and I enjoyed each mouthful.

"I am fearful of what might happen to us. Will any of the men on the boat assail our womanhood? Or will they leave us alone?"

"I think we will be safe until we are sold because virgins bring a better price." I don't know where I had heard it, but it made sense to me.

Carabel laughed, and then grew silent, eating a piece

of cheese and a date.

I wondered what caused her to laugh. I wanted to know but did not ask. After beginning slowly, I ate hungrily and became drowsy. I took a blanket, wrapped myself, and lay down as best I could. Carabel reclined next to me.

I woke up, feeling something was not right and found my blanket sopping wet and water pooled on the floor. Carabel was asleep and she roused as well. "The boat is leaking!" she shrieked.

"Help! Someone come help us. We are soaking wet down here!"

I heard nothing except the swishing of water and the whirring sound of wind. I stood up and went to our door. It opened when I turned the latch. We were not locked in as I had supposed. I motioned to Carabel to come with me. We crept up the steps into the darkness. At first, I saw no men on the deck, and I wondered where they all were. Of course, there could be another cabin. "Angus!" My voice was swallowed by the wind buffeting my face. No moon or stars were visible. The boat pitched and rocked, making it difficult to stand.

"It is too dark." Carabel stumbled and went back to our cabin.

I held onto whatever I could find on deck to steady myself and made my way forward, stepping over sleeping men, until I got to the place where the captain was steering. He did not see or hear me as he was at the helm and intent on handling sails. When he saw me, he said, "Get down below, woman, or this wind will take you off to sea. I am bringing the sails down entirely with the help of crewmen."

I held onto a large rope coil and did not heed his order.

He let go for a moment and shouted something to crewmen. Angus came, rubbing his eyes. When he saw me, he rushed to me, grabbed my arms, and pulled me toward our cabin.

"There is water down there. I came to tell someone. We are drowning in our beds."

He growled at me, "A little water will not hurt you. Now get back there, or I will tie you women to each other. How would you like that?" He shoved me, so I almost fell when we got to the door.

"You!" I said, but stopped, as I realized any words I uttered would be futile. I was fearful and terribly aggrieved with my situation.

Carabel sat on a cushion with her legs crossed under her so her feet were not on the wet floor. I sat on the other damp cushion and left my wet blanket on the floor.

"I wonder where we are," Carabel said.

"And where we are going?"

"We are too far out to sea for me to swim to safety anywhere." Carabel sounded as if she stifled sobs.

"I often dreamed of traveling to some foreign land, but this was not what I had in mind." I sighed.

I worried the ship would falter, and we would all

drown in the sea. I felt ill as we were buffeted by storm waves but did not lose the contents of my stomach. Carabel became sick, clutched her middle, and vomited into the stone jar. She wiped her mouth with a corner of her wet blanket. I wondered if we would get fresh blankets and if someone would come bail the water from our floor. How could they possibly hope to get a good price for two young women who were sick from the motion of the sea?

A miserable bit of time passed in which I asked a hopefully forgiving Lord to not remember all the things I had done wrong in the past. I had been a willful little girl who often gave my family grief. I remembered how Jesus spoke about having faith. I had faith I would be forgiven and rescued. At last, the sea calmed some, but I could not sleep. I kept striving for a solution to my imprisonment.

After several hours, I tried the door and found it still unsecured. I crept up and saw it was daylight. The sunrise on the water made a glorious golden path from the edge of the sea to where we were. I wondered if I now had a small insight into what Uncle Elias had told us about how the Creator God had felt when he saw His world and said it was very good. I marveled at its radiance and went the last step onto the deck. Now the wind was calm as was the sea, and I breathed in cool fresh air like none I had inhaled before.

I did not want to startle the captain, so I was quiet. As if he sensed my presence, he turned toward me and said, "A wonderful sight! I never tire of seeing it." I understood his Aramaic and Philistine dialect mixed words.

"I have never been at sea before. It is beautiful to behold this morning." I ventured closer to him. He was about the age of my brother or a little older. "Have you sailed all night without sleep?" I saw sails billowing softly in a pleasant waft of air.

"Yes, the wind pushed us off course, so I had to remain and not put the boat in the hands of a less skilled mariner. My men drew oars for a time when the sails had to be down or ruin in the punishing wind. You may come closer if you wish, as the sea is calm."

When I stood to one side behind him, I could see how he handled the sails and steering. Men on deck helped with billowing sails. "One has a rip, but it will be alright until we get to Egypt."

"I can sew, if you need someone to mend it," I said. I felt a cool breeze sway my robe. My wet sandals were drying. A deep abiding presence was with me, and my fear was beginning to subside.

"Thank you, no, at least for now I do not need your sewing skills."

I went to see how Carabel was doing. She sat on her cushion rubbing her eyes. "Where did you go?'

"I was on deck watching the captain and crewmen handle the boat. I heard them say we are going to Egypt. At least now we have a destination, but I don't know how long it will take us to get there."

"I will go up and ask them," Carabel said.

"The sea is lovely this morning. I will go with you." We went to talk with the captain, and when we came on deck, Angus and other men were up as well. Carabel did not speak but looked at the calm sea with a pleasant smile on her face. We both took deep breaths of sea air. I took a good look at our ship. It had a bird head carved at the bow and a bird tail appearance at the stern. I smelled the faint aroma of grain or hay. It was larger than I had thought at first and might have had some cargo aboard below the deck. Crewmen had been asleep on deck when I had come up the first time, but now all were busy. I saw Angus.

"Angus, our cabin is still wet, and we are thirsty and hungry," I said.

"I will get food for you in a short while," he said.

The captain was speaking to them in a language I could only understand in part. A crew member took over for him, and the captain went somewhere below. Angus opened a wooden trunk on the deck and reached inside. He came to us with a flask and some flatbread. "Go below to eat," he said.

"Your little flower wants to stay on deck where it is drier," I said.

He turned away and did not order us to go. Carabel and I sat on the cool planks in the warm sunlight eating bread and drinking watered wine from the flask. I felt almost free, but in my heart, I knew I was far from it. Everyone seemed more relaxed than when we first boarded.

Days passed. Carabel and I were allowed to come on deck. Our cabin had a damp floor, but no longer pooled water. We brought our blankets on deck to dry. Some crewmen leered unseemly at us but most kept a distance. Angus said, "Go below, women," but we lingered.

One of the deck crew, a handsome young man with thick arm muscles and wavy brown hair pulled back in a thong came near. "Which one of you would like to come down below with me? I have a dry blanket and a full flask of wine." He looked directly at me with dark glinting eyes and stroked his trimmed beard with his left hand. His face, especially his nose, reminded me of Roman guards.

Carabel and I were completely still. I looked past him to see if Angus or the captain was anywhere he could see us. If Angus knew of the man's forbidden behavior, the deckhand would be in chains.

I thought of screaming. No one was near, so I quickly decided we must protect ourselves. I nodded to Carabel, who nodded back, then I said to him, "Come closer. Where are you from as you speak perfect Aramaic?"

He knelt on one knee next to me, breathing heavily. The sunlight shone on his high, tanned forehead. Carabel locked eyes with me. In a quick move, we both stood and pushed him at the same time sending him sprawling onto the deck. We hurried, and ran below, not sure if he followed. Carabel and I stood with our backs braced against the door. We waited, life pulse pounding, afraid to breathe.

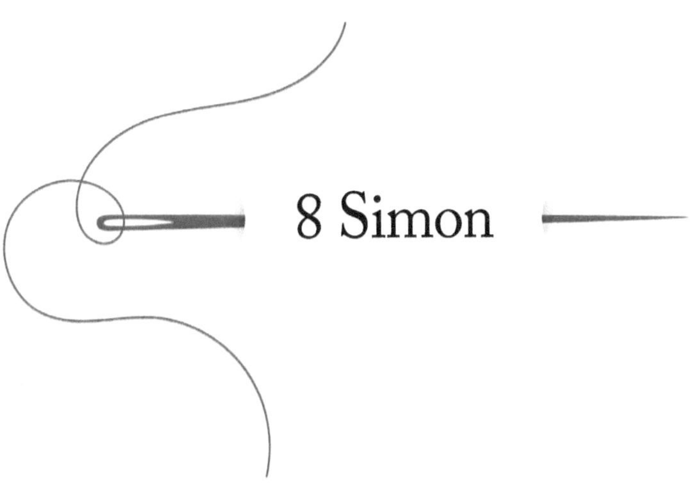

8 Simon

The human spirit can endure sickness; but a broken spirit – who can bear?

Proverbs 18:14

Lemuel and I trudged Mount Olive trail, our little bells tinkling a warning we were unclean. Lazarus met us halfway up. I saw him coming, and we kept our distance from him. "Lazarus, good to see you, but do not come any closer. How are you and your lovely sisters?"

"I am sorely vexed. Mary has gone somewhere and we cannot find her. I was hoping Jesus could help as she often trails after him and his followers even though she has been forbidden. He has gone to Galilee, and I hope she is with him, but I fear she is not. I am going to look for her until I find her. Have you seen her?"

"Days ago. I heard her singing as she went down the trail. One night I heard some people going on the trail around the mount side. It sounded like a donkey pulling a cart. It could have been a farmer with goods to sell or trade. Except for my friend Lemuel and the stonecutters, I have seen no one up here. We were in Jerusalem for a short time today. I am very sorry Mary is missing. She is a lovely young woman and needs protection."

"I am hoping for a miracle from my friend Jesus. He heals people of demons and restores sight to the blind. When he returns I will ask him to find Mary and to heal you and your friend."

"I have already tried the dog blood and goat blood cures and had no change in my condition," Lemuel said.

"He does not use any of those things. He heals by some divine means not known to me, but it is mystical, prayerful, and I believe his power is from YHWH." Lazarus kept his distance.

"He is a rabbi, and I am sure he is very busy with his followers who learn from him. I would like to be healed, but I do not want to trouble the man." I felt miserable after the day in Jerusalem and only wanted to slip into our secluded place beneath the gnarled old tree above the tombs and drink wine. I hoped Ott had brought us food and wine, or would as the sun set.

"As you wish, but I think if you listened to Jesus, you would welcome the chance to be healed by him. His power is from on high."

Lemuel stood by without speaking, and I could tell he was interested, but doubtful. I had known Jesus and his family since he was a young boy, and though he was wise beyond his years, I doubted the rumors of his powers.

"I must be on my way to Jerusalem before the sun sets," Lazarus said. His voice was plaintive, sad.

"Thank you for speaking with us. I hope you find Mary soon. Martha must be worried sick."

I was very troubled about Mary. She was a happy friendly young woman, and it would be so dreadful if she was never found. As for myself, I had given up hope of being healed. Lemuel and I veered off the trail and cut through the brushy area toward our regular spot. I did not speak until we were well away from Lazarus. I hoped I had not already inflicted my neighbor when I had first come back from travels. When we had visited then, and I showed what I thought to be insect bites, he had rightly suggested I might have leprosy.

Lemuel and I settled in our usual place under the gnarled tree and watched the stonecutters leaving for the day. A new craftsman had been at work on a façade in front of the cavern. It was taking the shape of Greek-style architecture with columns. He had only started, but one could see the general outline. I felt proud I had contracted this skillful crew.

What good was pride in the work now? I shook my head as the cruelty of my situation once more consumed me. I tried to keep my thoughts from finding a quick way to take my life. Lemuel distracted me from my murderous thoughts when he spoke.

"What did you think of our outing today?"

I shook my head, and stared at Lemuel, not wanting to speak, but finally did. "I thought it was demeaning and horrible, and I hated seeing the man who would have been my father-in-law. Abner thought he was being kind by throwing small coins to us, but I felt even worse after he did."

Lemuel nodded in agreement. "I think I see your servant down below who brings us the basket of food and drink."

"Thank you, Ott," I called to him. He looked my direction but could not see me.

"Good evening, Master," Ott said.

I wondered how much longer I could afford to pay Ott and his wife. How long would I be able to keep running my business? I felt heartsick and sat with my head in my hands. My body was frightfully sore, yet in some parts, I had lost feeling entirely. My spirit was at the lowest ebb it had ever been. I waited until the last craftsman had left for the day, and then said to Lemuel, "If you are hungry go get the basket for us."

Lemuel stood, waiting for me to join him. When I remained seated, he went down to get the basket and brought it up. Usually, I uncovered it, anxious for any word from Judith's father. Today, I said, "Uncover it and eat whatever you want. I am not hungry."

Lemuel nodded, sat, and took the cloth off the basket. I saw tucked in one side of the provisions, a neatly rolled parchment. Lemuel saw it, too but did not touch it. He handed me a round of bread. I took it, but did not break it to eat. I did not reach for the parchment. I dreaded what I would read. I hated my days, and could not think of food. Lemuel offered me a wineskin.

I untied the cord binding the neck and lifted it to my lips. It was sweet to my tongue and warmed my insides as I drank. I wondered idly and sadly at what Lazarus had imparted to me about his sister's disappearance. I wished I could help him look for her.

Emboldened by wine, I pulled the parchment out of the basket and tried to read it in the fading light, yet I knew what it would say. Since I had leprosy, Judith and I would not marry, and they would keep the bride's price I had paid as I had specified. She would be free to marry someone else. Perhaps Abner would begin with words of deep regret. I didn't care anymore, at least I told myself I didn't care. I only wished I could have seen my beautiful Judith once more. It was not to be. No tears, I wept deeply inside where it burned. I tossed the unread parchment back into the basket.

I had not doubted my faith until leprosy had devastated me. If there even was a YHWH, he hated me. I wanted to speak to him, tell him of my adherence to his laws, my good attributes, benevolent deeds, contributions, sacrifices, and my honesty in a thriving business. I said aloud, "Why am I here? How can a just God find fault in me? How can he treat me so cruelly? What is it I have done wrong? If there is anything I need to do, please tell me and I will right the wrong."

"Simon, you have not done any wrong I see, and neither have I. Life is made difficult for some of us, while others go unscathed. It is unfair."

"Some who are inherently evil, who do not keep faith and commandments, have riches, land, wives, and children. They go unpunished despite unlawful practices. There is not a judicious Lord or it would not be allowed." The sky had blackened, and I saw no moon or stars. Growl! I saw a flash, and I heard a rumbling, which soon grew louder as lightning streaked across the sky. "Is this your answer, YHWH?" I yelled into the flashing sky and thunder and shook my fist, as the rain pelted my half-sore and partly numb face. Where there was still any feeling, it was as if holes were being bored into my skin. I shivered and curled into a ball of misery. Lemuel grabbed my hand and the basket. "Come, let us take shelter in your workman's tomb."

I scarcely remember the muddy, sliding steps we made to get to cover. My life pulse beat rapidly. Once inside the cave, it smelled musty, chalky, and earthy. We said nothing. I could hear our quick shallow breathing. I chuckled softly. "Thank you, Lemuel, I needed to inspect their work, didn't I?" My lungs breathed in dust and my feet scuffed sand and stone.

"Good if you can see in the dark, Simon."

I had never asked what Lemuel had done to earn his living before he got leprosy. All he had shared was about his brother having taken over responsibility for his wife and children. I thought to ask but it mattered little right now.

I must have dozed off to sleep. I dreamed of little Mary, my neighbor. She was calling out to me to come help her. As I awakened, I did not know where I was. The storm had passed and it was quiet, except for Lemuel snoring fitfully beside me. I crept out into the damp, chilly night. Stars, like jewels, dotted the black sky, and a crescent moon shone.

Alone, I was so very alone. I, Simon, who had had everything my heart desired—a good business reputation, men who respected me, a nice home, and the promise of a beautiful wife. I would have shaken my fist at the sky again, at YHWH who had allowed the calamity of leprosy to steal my life, but I stopped and stood in awe at his creation. After all, I was a mere man, and if he had created mankind, there were unfathomable numbers of us. "If you are there, YHWH, keep little Mary safe." I saw the faint light appearing in the sky and went into the cave to wake Lemuel. Even as we scurried up the hill, I heard workmen coming. I braced myself for another day of misery.

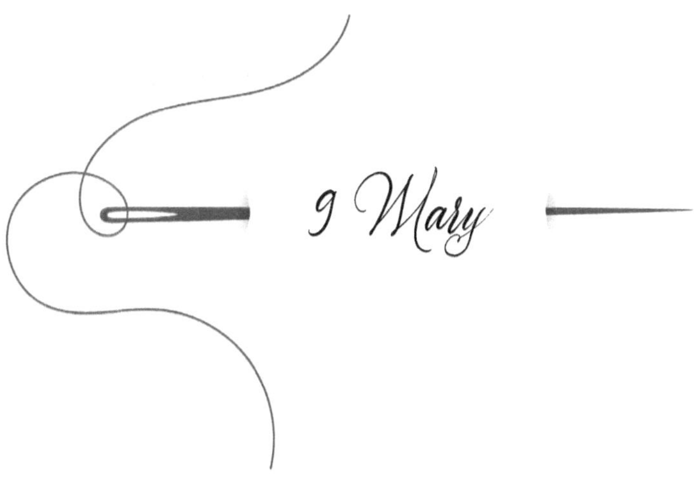

9 Mary

See, O Lord, how distressed I am; my stomach churns, my heart is wrung within me, because I have been rebellious. In the street, the sword bereaves; in the house, it is like death.

Lamentations 1:20

When I heard excited exclamations from the ship's crew, I knew we were almost to land somewhere. My stomach churned with dread of what might lay ahead for me. We came to the port, where there appeared to be a bustling town. The clean scent of the sea air which had been with us gave way to odors of people and rich spices and rotting fish.

As we disembarked, Angus spoke with a man clad in a blue richly embroidered cloak who was waiting for him. Carabel and I were escorted off the boat and onto a path of flat stones. Other boats were being unloaded and people were walking nearby. Many men were dressed in fine robes, turbans, jeweled, embroidered, colorful, or plain, and other people almost in tatters. They were black-skinned, brown, tan, or white. I had never seen such an array of people.

The man summoned two eunuchs, who came to us. One whose green eyes were crossed, took Carabel by the hand. The other took my hand with his large soft hand. "I am Sangie," he said. He was only a little taller than me and had a sweet round face with fine white hair on his cheeks, blue eyes, and thin light-colored shoulder-length hair. He smelled of clean spices.

"Where are you taking me?" I asked.

He giggled in a high pitch, shook his head, and offered me his hand. I slipped my hand from his light grasp and walked beside him. I wondered if he was deaf or could not understand my language or didn't want to tell me. We went a short way and were met by a tall man in a tan cloak who stood by a fine horse-drawn carriage. Carabel and I were each lifted up to the carrier which had red cushioned seats and a plain fabric roof. We glanced at each other as we settled on the cushions. "My guard is named Ulta and yours is Sangie," Carabel said. The two eunuchs sat behind the carriage driver who led the two black horses.

"Guards?" I wondered what role these persons had where we were concerned. Soon, the horses kicked up dust and we were going faster than I had ever traveled before. I held my breath at first but settled and looked at the vast desert expanse on either side. We were in Egypt, but I did not know where. We did not stop. Before nightfall, we approached a large building where we had to cross a bridge over a deep ditch or dry stream. At a tall wide gate, the horses stopped, and the two eunuchs alit and came to the back where Carabel and I sat. Sangie motioned for me to stand, and he took both my hands so I could get down. Ulta helped Carabel. We stood while the driver was paid by a gatekeeper. And as the carriage left, dust trailed behind. Reality of my dire situation once more set in and I cringed.

The olive-skinned sentry opened the gate for us. He wore shoes laced to his knees into which were tucked brown trousers. His plain tan cloak had slits for his bare arms to be free, and he had a sword mounted in a sling at his waist. Once we were through the tall wood gate, there was a door leading to a hallway. While the sun shone outside, it was somewhat dark inside as only small upper windows let in light. My life pulse quickened its beat, and my arms prickled with fear. I had been sold into slavery. Would my master be mean or kind? What would I have to do? Had YHWH abandoned me? I should not think such thoughts. I still had faith Jesus or my brother would come find me.

Carabel was led by Ulta to our left down a hallway, and I continued with Sangie until there was a short rise of two flat stone steps going into a room. The floor was polished stone, and partially covered with a many-colored floral-patterned carpet. Sunlight streamed in. Sangie ushered me inside and gestured with a sweep of his hand as if he were inviting me into his home. He smiled broadly and giggled. A large luxurious red plush bed was in the center. There were beautifully crafted stone tables and shiny wine-red cushions on either side. I had not ever experienced such a large furnished and decorated room. A small window to the outside brought in warm fresh air. I walked to a lower small window and saw an endless terrain of desert with few plants. Nearer, in the courtyard below, there was statuary with symbols. Benches of stone were situated in the shade areas where date palms were growing. Two young women in plain natural-colored long tunics strolled there. One held a tray with a red clay dish on it and the other carried a sack.

I looked back at Sangie, who appeared pleased at my open-mouthed reaction. He drew aside a curtain in the corner of the room to reveal some brightly colored garments. "These are for you," he said, in halting Aramaic. He bowed slightly, and I saw a piece of jewelry on a chain glint at his neck. I wanted to ask him what it was, but he left the room quickly.

When he returned, he brought a cup and a small ewer of drinking water he placed on a square table. And he had a covered container for me to use to relieve myself which he placed in another corner concealed by a plain linen curtain. I had never been so attended in my life. He was not a guard, as Carabel had said, but a personal servant for me. "Thank you," I said. "Is your master as kind as you are?"

"Master Arthrimian is kind to me. You will meet him tomorrow evening, I think."

"Does this place have a name?" I was glad Sangie could hear and understand me.

"House of Arthrimian." Sangie bowed and left me. I was alternately too warm and then chilled, worrying about my fate. I wondered about a master who was nice to a servant, but how would he behave toward me? I wanted to escape before I found out. I had heard stories of masters who did not treat their slaves kindly, and even beat them.

I pondered on his words and looked out the window in my room at the vast barren wilderness. My stomach was queasy as I could not think of a way to escape where there was no place to hide if I left. I was sitting on a cushion drinking a cup of water when Sangie returned with a tray of food.

Fish, vegetables, a stew, cheese, bread, a pomegranate, and dates were there for me to eat. While it looked and smelled wonderful, I had little appetite. At sea, I had subsisted on dry bread, dates, a little goat cheese, and water. He put a cloth on the table and gave me a plate and spoon. I bowed my head and thanked YHWH for the food and for bringing me here safely. I put a large sumptuous date in my mouth and chewed slowly. Someone had removed the pit before serving it. Before he left, Sangie bowed and I saw his necklace bore a shiny ankh. I only knew what it was from a discussion Lazarus had with his friends one day. They drew an outline of it in the sand and told how the Egyptians used it as a sign for El. Was not El, or Elohim, another name for YHWH? They discussed whether or not it was true, but none of them knew for certain.

Sangie came to see if I needed anything else. I wanted to ask him about the small ankh but decided to wait. It was too much to wish he worshipped YHWH as I did. I wondered how long he had been in the service of Master Arthrimian. I asked, "Am I permitted to walk in the courtyard?"

"I can arrange it, but someone will have to go with you."

"May I go now?"

Sangie raised a hand and left. He came back quickly. "Yes, I can take you for a walk while we still have daylight."

He led me outside, and we strolled in the courtyard

among the statuary of lions, birds, and dogs. Some steles were there with odd carvings of the ankh, the sun, eyes, animals, or a staff of some kind on them. Except for a few date trees which cast a long dark image, we walked in waning sunlight. The shadows of the steles had elongated and deepened. I said, "I have had a nice walk, we can go back inside." I had a deep sense of emptiness inside, was tired, and missed my family.

He nodded and escorted me to my room. I saw no one else and wondered how Carabel was doing. "Is Carabel alright?"

Sangie nodded, and said, "She will meet Master Arthrimian tomorrow at dinner as you will." Even though I had been in bright sunlight moments ago, I realized the sun was about to set. I prayed in my heart we would be alright. I tried to think of all the prayers I had heard from Jesus and my Uncle Elias. I quoted his blessing to reassure myself. "The Lord bless you and keep you, the Lord lift up his countenance upon you, look upon you with favor and give you peace." It was not the same as when Jesus or my uncle said it, but it did give me a small measure of peace.

I was very tired and ready for the plush bed in my room. I longed to wash my feet, but no basin had been provided, and Sangie had left. I worried about Carabel but soon calmed, as I occupied my mind with a time past when Jesus had visited us in Bethany.

***

Martha hummed softly as she stirred a savory lamb stew she cooked in a large kettle suspended over the fire in our hearth. Bread aroma wafted as I brought it in from the oven outside. We had swept our packed dirt floors until they shone. I swept out front, too excited to sit still until I saw Jesus strolling up our pathway. I almost swooned at the sight of him, wanted so much to be near him and listen to his every word.

"Please come in." I felt flushed in my face as I spoke to him.

"Little Mary, you are so kind. Lazarus told me you were with him when the crowd followed me to the river. I am sorry I did not see you then."

"It was exciting to be there. I met a nice old man who sells rugs and things. While I could not hear you, people around me were saying favorable things about you. Many adore you for the miracles you have been doing."

"They are not my miracles, but those of my father YHWH."

I went to get a basin of water and a towel to wash his feet. Lazarus took over and bathed his friend's feet. I would have liked to touch him.

More people crowded into our house, and Martha prepared to feed them. I found a spot near Jesus so I could hear his every word.

He stood with his right arm stretched out in front of him.

Someone asked, "What is the Kingdom of Heaven

like if I am sinful, and someday I die? May I hope to go there? What will happen if I am sorry for all my wrongdoings?"

"Suppose a woman has ten silver coins and loses one. Does she not light a lamp, sweep the house and search carefully until she finds it? And when she finds it she calls her friends and neighbors together and says, 'Rejoice with me; I have found my lost coin. In this same way, I tell you, there is rejoicing in the presence of the angels of God over one sinner who repents.'"

He continued to speak. I tried to take in everything, but my mind kept drifting to what it would be like to be embraced by him, and have him gaze into my eyes. He was a wise and good man we had known for some years. As I sat there enraptured among the listeners, Martha was bustling about in the kitchen, stirring stew and putting plates out. She gave me the sisterly look, which meant she wanted my help. When I kept my seat, she asked Jesus to tell me to get up and help her. When she asked him to admonish me, I was embarrassed. He told her I had chosen wisely and honored him by listening to him. Although he chided her for not taking time to sit and visit, he thanked her and acknowledged her service to him and his followers by her dutiful meal preparation. "We all have gifts," he said. Then he went into the kitchen area and began to help Martha put food on the table, beginning with the bread which he later broke for all to eat. He cupped his fingers on his right hand to beckon James and Philip to help. Some men shook their heads at their Rabbi's actions. I got up to help as well.

Would I ever see Martha again? How I missed her, even her scolding me for being idle. If I ever saw her again, I would try to help more. I missed Lazarus, Jesus, and our neighbor Simon. Simon traveled frequently, but when he came home he sometimes brought little gifts for us. He was wise and kind and I liked him.

I slept fitfully with many questions in my mind. Would I ever see my family and Jesus again? Perspiration beaded on my forehead. I knew I ought to have faith, but I dreaded tomorrow. What would Master Arthrimian be like?

10 Simon

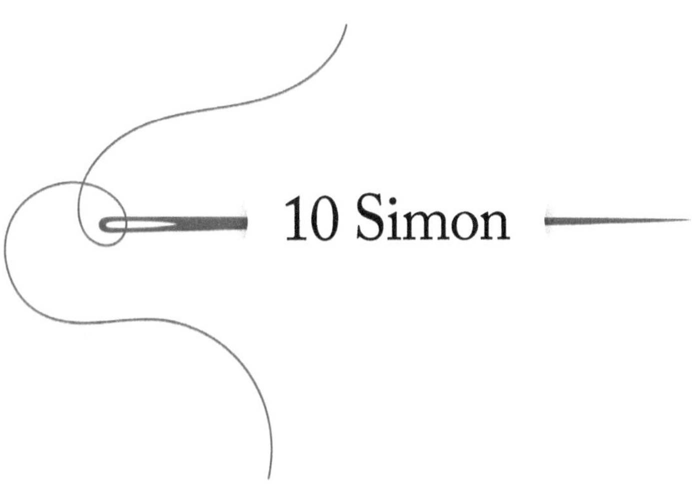

I lift up my eyes to the hills—
from where will my help come?

Psalm 121:1

I reached into the damp basket, trying to find the parchment Abner had sent. I asked Lemuel, "Did you remove the parchment roll?"

"No, Simon, it was there before the storm hit. Is it gone?"

"Must be here somewhere." I felt agitated. I moved each wet bread round, the block of cheese, and a handful of dates, but it was not there. Then I began to search the ground around us, but did not find it. "Maybe it fell out inside the cave, but I cannot go back and retrieve it with the workers there."

I looked toward Jerusalem as was my habit. The air was fresh and I lazed, as there was nothing else to occupy my mind or my time. I felt strangely calm and wondered if I was healing. Lemuel went for a short stroll away from me, and I was left to my thoughts, which today were not as dire or self-murderous as they had been due to loathing my body condition.

I heard the men talking as they took short breaks outside the cavern they were digging. "He healed a blind man and one who was deaf and could not speak. I wonder how he does his magic medicine."

"Sorcery or Beelzebul, it has to be," one said. "I'd stay away from that long-haired young man. No good comes out of Nazareth." Laughter ensued. They had been in the area long enough to hear local reports, and had formed an opinion about Jesus.

I supposed they were talking about Jesus, the one I was well acquainted with, whom Lazarus wanted me to see. I had seen and heard Jesus in the company of a group of his young followers and Lazarus, but never taken him seriously. He was a rabbi, followed by some lively young men who had mostly been fishermen, probably too poor to have their families put them under the tutelage of a rabbi. The workers were on to other subjects concerning their progress on the dig. The foreman called them back to work inside.

Lemuel returned, and I related the men's comments to him. He nodded. "Jesus is not a sorcerer. Maybe we should give the man a chance. I have faith, and if Jesus is from YHWH, I believe he can make us well. I am willing to give him the opportunity. You said you have met him, and your neighbor knows him well."

"I have known the teacher in the past. I suppose I should think about it."

"I looked for your message from Abner but did not find it. I thought it could have blown somewhere in the wind. We must go into the cave tonight to see if it is there."

"You are a good friend. I suppose I do not need to read the note as it will tell me what I already know," I said. I stopped speaking as I heard a voice echoing almost as if singing, as people were coming up Mount Olive.

I listened to the words, "Believe in YHWH, also believe in the Son of Man. Love one another as I have loved you." His voice was beautiful, and he was going toward Bethany where Lazarus lived. I heard other voices and realized it was Jesus, and these would be the followers of the rabbi. I smiled, something I had not done for many days. I was glad Lazarus knew him well. Since his good friend Jesus was back, perhaps Mary had come home.

I almost called out but remembered I was unclean, and could not hope to be in the presence of anyone. Sadness crept over me. I had missed my chance to have Lazarus speak to Jesus for me. I stayed among the tombs and sipped wine from my flask.

Something caught my eye as I sat contemplating my fate, a bit of white caught in a briar down below. I scooted down on my backside, as it was too steep to walk there. When I got to it, I could reach it, but the parchment was entangled in thorns. My hands were full of sores anyway, so what could it harm to put a few more on my fingers? Both my skin and the parchment tore as I grabbed a corner of the note. When I brought it out where I could see it, the ink had blurred from getting wet and mingled with drops of my blood.

I saw the remnants of Abner's seal. While the writing was mostly unclear, some words stood out, "regret to release you." There were a few more ink marks, but I couldn't make out the words. I wondered why I had bothered to read it, except I was accustomed to finalizing any business transaction, whether it was to proceed, cancel or alter terms. When I settled back beside Lemuel, he asked, "Did you love the woman?"

"I loved what I saw as she was beautiful, and I knew

she was from an upstanding, devout family."

"It is not the same as love."

"What do you mean? When parents arrange marriages for their daughters, it has more to do with economics and status than love. Perhaps if one is fortunate, love and mutual respect develop."

"I suppose so." Lemuel sat quietly, arms folded.

"Did you love your wife who is now your brother's wife?"

"Yes. We grew up in the same neighborhood, and I was always fond of her. I played with her and her brothers. After we were of age, of course, she and I could no longer play. I saw her from afar and stole away to watch her when I knew she was going for water with her mother. I loved her, and our parents mutually decided we could marry."

"Does it break your heart to know she is in your brother's arms?"

"I try not to think about it. She is better off in his home and under his caring protection, and so are our children with their cousins." A tear slipped down his scarred cheek, and he did not brush it away.

Jesus was nearby, and I heard him say, "Do you believe in me? Do you believe I can heal?"

"How does he know we are here?' Lemuel whispered to me. "He cannot see us."

"Answer him," I said. "Lazarus surely told him where we sit."

Lemuel cleared his throat, and called fervently and

clearly, "Yes, Jesus, I have faith in you and I believe you can heal me. If it pleases you, I want to be healed by you."

"Be healed." Jesus's voice rang out like a decree. "Wash in the Pool of Siloam. Go to the Temple and make a thank offering. Then go home to your wife and family. You are well."

Lemuel stood, his mouth agape. I was amazed as some scabs from his face and hands fell to the earth and disappeared among the pebbles. "Simon, look, I am becoming well, now you must answer him, and allow Jesus to heal you."

I waited, hoping Jesus would speak again, but he did not. "Go, Lemuel, you have much to be thankful for. Hopefully, you now can see your wife and children."

"Alright, I will see you soon, Simon!" Lemuel hurried away, too excited to look back.

I was left, staring down at the tombs as my friend rushed off to do everything Jesus had asked him to do. I was a proud man, accustomed to paying for services, and did not want charity. Jesus had not asked for anything for himself, only a thank offering to be given to the Temple. I paid my Temple dues regularly. Jesus did not speak again. Everything around me was quiet.

Alone, I had even more time to ponder my circumstances. Leprosy had deprived me of marriage to Judith, a lovely woman from a good family. I supposed it was the way it had to be. Could I humble myself and crawl to the man who was curing people? If I were to be healed, would there be any chance Abner would not already have made arrangements for his daughter to wed another man? What if Lemuel was not completely healed? In fact, how could he have been? I only saw some scabs come loose from his hands and face. No, it was probably only temporary. He had scabs for a while and they were probably ready to come off after the recent drenching in rain. I would wait and see.

Later, Ott left a basket of food again, with enough bread and wine for two men. I laughed. It would be great if I had an appetite. I had forgotten to put the basket with empty wineskins where he could get it. Never mind I had more than one basket and wineskins. When I retrieved the basket, I saw a rolled parchment, but it was not from Abner.

As soon as it grew light the next morning, I unrolled it. I read some scrawled words, "Why did you not heed the words of Jesus? He would have healed you." It was from Lazarus.

I did not know what to do, or how to respond to my friend's note. Perhaps if I knew Lemuel was completely well, I could allow myself to answer with words of faith I did not feel. It would only be Lemuel's faith. Would it suffice?

Clearly, Lazarus was disappointed in me. I knew I should have more faith, should put myself into the hands of Jesus, and tell him what he wanted to hear. I decided it was worth a try whenever next time his voice would echo on the Mount Olive Trail.

I had no ink or parchment to reply to Lazarus, so I

decided to use the parchment he had sent, and try to find something with which to scratch out a short reply. There was a small twig, and I used dirt to scratch out a line I hoped would convey I had at least gotten the message. I put it along with depleted flasks into the basket to return.

I was alone in the night and not afraid. I missed Lemuel and wondered how his family was reacting to seeing him well again if he was healed. Did Lemuel's brother try to keep his wife for himself? I felt sad and happy for my friend and wondered idly how my stonecutters were doing. I occupied my mind with business and remembered a shipment of supplies was soon arriving at the port. Ordinarily, I would travel there to oversee and account for the number of containers of goods I had ordered to be sold and traded in Jerusalem in many of the stalls I owned. The goods were marketed and sold by people I hired to manage the products and sales. I allowed widowed women who managed a stall to keep the entire profit. It was the right thing to do when they had no other way to feed their family. It was all so different now. I wanted to get word to someone to oversee the shipment, to account for all I had ordered. Ott would not be capable, and I thought of Lazarus but did not want to risk being close to him to transact business. Lemuel was one who could possibly handle the shipment for me, but I did not know how to contact him. He would not come back here if he was truly healed.

Any thought of getting Jesus to heal me the next

time I heard him disappeared from my mind. Perhaps tonight I would die under the gnarled old tree. I slumped back into my despair and gulped a big swallow of wine. I tilted the flask to my mouth and wine spilled out and soaked my beard. I loathed myself.

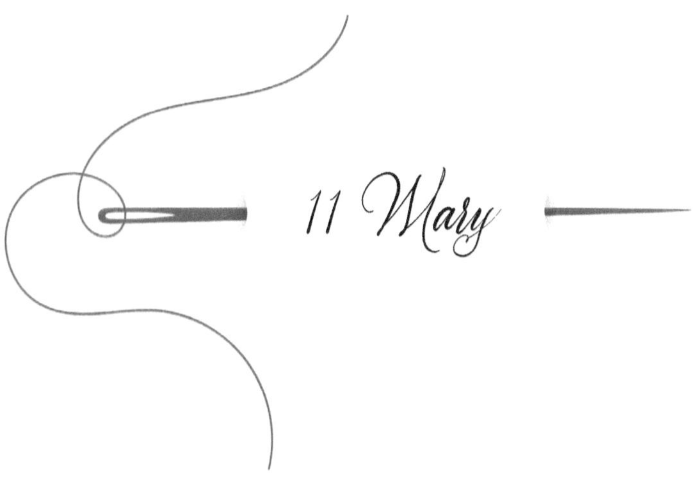

You who live in the shelter of the Most High, who abide in the shadow of the Almighty will say to the Lord, 'My refuge and my fortress; my God in whom I trust.'

Psalm 91:1-2

I dreamed of Jesus and my brother being in the room watching over me throughout the night. Neighbor Simon wore a torn garment as if he was grieving, and I wondered why. They were only dreams but gave me concern as well as hope and faith.

In the morning, sunlight streamed in my window. I arose and stared at the vast desert. I saw in the distance a small green patch and wondered how far away it was. The courtyard below was completely enclosed, so the only exit would be from the front gate. Safety from any enemies of Master Arthrimian was provided partly by the ditch and one locked gate in front.

Sangie tapped lightly on my door and came in with a tray of fruit and bread, and a flask of watered wine. "Did you sleep well?"

"Yes, I did. I feel the need to wash myself."

"When you have eaten your fill, I will take you to the bath."

"I am accustomed to a small basin of water and towel to wash my hands before I eat, and my feet when I enter the house."

"I will get water and towels for you next time you walk in the courtyard, but the place is not dirty."

After breakfast in my room, Sangie led me down some stone stairs to a pool inside the house. It was not a mikveh as we had for ritual cleansing, but a little larger. He gave me a towel. I was embarrassed as he undressed me, even though I could easily have done so myself. I went into the tepid water. It felt comforting to soak my body, and I stayed for a long time. Sangie did not rush me or leave me. He did not watch, but sat back with his hands cupped behind his head and closed his eyes.

Afterwards, he wrapped me in a plush white wool robe, and accompanied me to my room to dress for the day. "You will dress in different clothing for our master this evening," he said. I selected a plain long green cotton. I had never had a green garment in my life. It felt soft and comfortable. Sangie left me alone.

I had nothing to do. I was used to sewing or cleaning. Someone tapped on the door, and a young woman about my height with braided dark brown hair, wearing a long, plain tunic entered. She greeted me in a language I did not understand. I realized she was there to sweep the floor and dust the tables.

"Thank you, I can clean my room. I am Mary."

"Myanna," she said and smiled. She removed my chamber pot from behind the curtain and brought it back empty. She cleaned the tiled floor, then bowed and left. Since I was not to clean rooms, I feared I was bought as a concubine companion for the Master Arthrimian. Was he old, young, or somewhere in between?

In the evening, a banquet had been laid on a long wooden table grander than any I had seen. The polished wood must have come from afar. I wore a plain simply embroidered linen tunic and light green silken scarf I had found among the garments provided for me. Cushions were on the floor, so people could eat comfortably, and even recline. I had never eaten at such a fine table with glass and ceramic tableware. Carabel came in escorted by Ulta who showed her a brown cushion opposite mine. She wore a fine pink tinted linen garment trimmed with sparkling jewels. There was an especially plump red plush cushion for Master Artherimian at the end where he would sit between us. No other guests seemed to be invited to the feast. Candles burned all about the room creating flickering eyes on the highly polished crockery.

Wine goblets were set and filled by the servants. Delicious aromas wafted in the air. Master Arthrimian came into the room. He wore a purple robe draped about himself and simple sandals. He stood and looked at Carabel and me, letting his dark eyes light first on her shiny waved hair and pleasant fair freckled face, then on me. He cleared his throat, "I am your Master Arthrimian, and I secured you both to be mine, to serve me as I have need. You will not see me very often as I am a busy man, but when you are summoned to my chambers, you must come. I see you are both young and inexperienced, and I may have you trained to serve me as I desire. I hope you will enjoy the meal with me." When he settled on the cushion, he turned to me and smiled behind his trimmed mustache and short black beard. Then he turned to Carabel.

"You have come from far away to be here. I trust you will like your surroundings. Is your room satisfactory? If it is not, please let your servants know and every effort will be made to keep you comfortable here." I did not understand all his words, but what I did hear is what I have quoted. His hair was dark and his skin ruddy and taut on his sculpted face. I noticed when he reached for his wine goblet his hands were not worn and calloused, but soft and clean, with gold rings on some of his fingers. He looked a little older than my brother Lazarus.

We remained on cushions on the floor, and the food was served on tan ceramic plates. He devoted most of his attention to the sumptuous food continually placed before us. Roast lamb, vegetables, grapes, pomegranates, cheeses, breads, and rich savory sauces. I was so nervous I ate little food but sat watching him. Carabel flirted with her eyes and plucked grapes from stems which she put into her mouth one at a time delicately removing seeds with her fingertips. He gave her his entire attention, and I felt grateful as I would probably have said something I would regret. She understood what he said, and responded to him. I was silent, and my insides clenched in knots.

When our meal was done, Sangie told me the master had selected Carabel to accompany him the rest of the evening. I worried about her and wondered if there was anything I could do to help her. I would not be seeing Arthrimian in his chambers until his next request for a woman. Sangie took my arm and accompanied me to my room where he turned down the cover on the bed. I removed the gown I had worn and hung it up even though I knew Sangie would do it. I kept on the light linen undergarment and tried to relax on the soft bed, curling into a ball with my knees to my chest. I was shaken by my captivity. I wanted to leave but did not know how or when I could. I got up and walked to the window to look out at the night sky bejeweled by many stars. Did Martha and Lazarus see the same lovely heavens? With God's direction, I hoped they were somehow on their way to find me.

I must not lose faith. There was so much about the world I did not know or understand. Cool night air wafted on my face as I stood there, alone and afraid. Even though I had eaten, I was hollow inside. When would I be able to escape? Would some unseen presence attend me? At this moment, I was frustrated, very much alone, and I wept quietly.

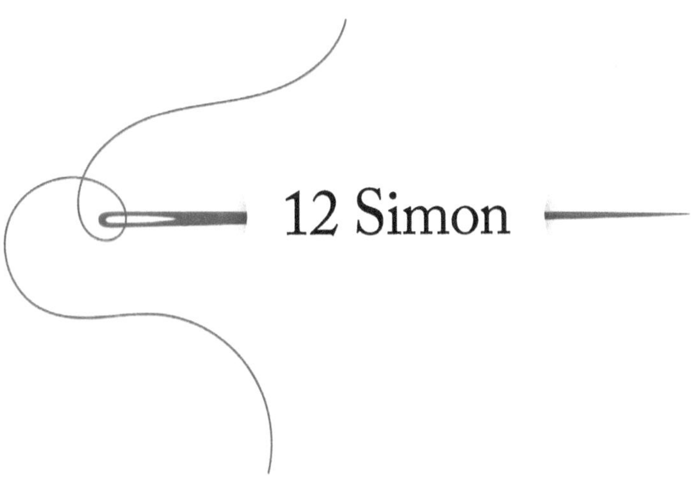

12 Simon

*O, Lord, God of my salvation, when at night I cry out in
your presence, let my prayer come before you; incline
your ear to my cry.*

Psalm 88:1–2

I slept fitfully and kept hearing an echo of a night bird in the trees. An eerie silence ensued. A rumble overhead awakened me and I knew it would rain. I didn't care. It felt good at first to have my body cooled by the rain drops. Parts of me did not feel anything. I fell asleep, and I dreamed. It could have been real for all I knew.

"What sin caused you to be afflicted with leprosy? Did you know a prostitute? How many? You must have been fraudulent in a business transaction," a formidable man said.

Abner was there mocking me. In his hand were two small coins. "Maybe you took advantage of someone, stole from one who could not defend himself. I am glad YHWH has punished you, and you have given up your claim for my daughter."

"I am innocent. I did none of those things, nor any ill. I am being treated unfairly," I protested. My voice was like the squeak of a small rodent.

"Where is your faith in YHWH?" My father's voice accused me.

"You cannot be speaking, Father, for you have gone to the dead some years ago. I pay my temple dues as you taught me." I shook my head.

"Unfaithful man!" It was the voice of Judith.

'I am sorely vexed. I don't deserve this torment. Go away from me, all of you," I said. I tore the sleeve of my tunic. Awakened, I became aware of my life pulse hammering in my chest. In spite of the rain, my whole body felt scorched as if in a hot sun. Ashes were all around me. I moved to sit up and realized it had been a miserable dream. There were no ashes. None of the people had been here accusing me. I grabbed the second wine flask from the basket, as I had emptied the first. I sipped it slowly. It did little to ease my painful thoughts.

I began to examine my life, my very existence. Was I a bad man, a greedy businessman? Had I looked at any woman lustfully? If I was guilty of anything at all, would there be a way to go back in time and atone for the wrongs? The answer I kept coming up with was the same; I could not go back and relive my past if I did fall short in my moral dealings with anyone. I could think of nothing I had done to deserve my terrible condition. As morning dawned I could not let go of the haunting dream. Had the accusers in my dream found fault? No, I had not visited prostitutes, not cheated or taken advantage of anyone, or stolen from anyone, and as for my faith, I attended synagogue, gave my dues at the temple, and I paid taxes. I was honest in my business transactions. Could YHWH find fault in me?

I listened for the men to come to the cavern to dig, but they didn't arrive. Perhaps they had finished the burial cave for the family. Was it the Sabbath? I had lost interest in what day of the week I had as each one was woefully the same. My Sabbath rest had begun with unrest, and while my body was reclined, my mind worked on many worries.

I drifted off to sleep in the afternoon. I heard the

voice of a young woman nearby and wondered who would be traipsing around on the Sabbath. She hummed a tune and stopped to make comments to herself. "Did you get soaked during the storm, or were you able to take shelter? I know you cannot speak, rabbit, and you look fine to me." She laughed. I hoped she would not come near me as I did not want to move from where I lay.

"Do not come near me. I am unclean." I jingled my little bell. Perhaps I was not alive at all.

"Neighbor Simon, is it you? Jesus was supposed to heal you. What happened?" Her soft voice faded.

In my delirium, I thought Mary spoke. I said, "Please do not trouble yourself concerning me. I am an old man and will die soon anyway. Have you returned to your sister and brother?"

"No, I am far away, away." Her voice trailed off like an echo.

I wished even now I could be tending to my business interests instead of being trapped in a leprous body. I wanted to help search for Mary. "Please stay away from me." I repeated my warning as I thought I heard someone move through the brush. How could she be far away and speaking to me at the same time? Startled, I sat up fully awake, and all I heard were tiny bird tweets. Another strange dream; it had been Mary, and she was not here.

After the troubling dreams, when I awakened I felt weaker than ever. I looked at the wet food basket which had some soggy bread, cheese, and figs ready to eat. When I picked up the bread, it crumbled into mush. I lost any appetite I had. There were only a few sips left in the wine flask. Never mind, a new basket would show up when Ott came.

But the next day, when the sun was almost set and the workmen had left, I did not see Ott. I wondered what had happened, but decided he had simply been delayed by some family matter. I thought about my friend Lemuel, hoped he was truly well, and he had been able to rejoin his wife and children without complications from his brother or anyone.

My whole body was worn out from the dream incidents. It had seemed real. I worried about Mary. If I were well, I would be helping Lazarus look for his young sister. Perhaps the miracle worker Jesus would bring her back when he returned once more from Galilee.

I munched on a bit of soggy cheese and a date, but without bread, it did not satisfy. Where could Ott be? I hoped he was not ill, or his family sick. As it grew dark, I decided to take a chance and creep to my house. Small vines on the path caused me to stumble, but I was able to catch myself. How stupid it was for a man like me to be crawling to his own home in the dark to find food. A night bird sounded nearby, startled me, and I tripped again. I berated myself. Why was I even going to look for food? I would probably die soon anyway, but who would touch my diseased body to bury it now Lemuel was healed and gone.

When I got to my home, I saw no lamplight in the window, so Ott must have retired early. I tossed pebbles again as I had done the last time I had come. No one responded. I went to my door and rapped on it, hoping to rouse him and his wife. I tried the latch, and the door opened, so he had not secured it on the inside as he usually did at night. I called, "Ott, it is Simon! Are you doing alright? Is someone ill?" My voice fell flat. I listened. I had an awful sense of foreboding as I stepped inside. "Ott, it is Simon. Are you here?"

I entered cautiously, lest there had been an intruder who lurked. It was dark and dank and did not smell like my home. I wondered desperately what could be the matter. What else would go wrong in my life? I found the oil lamp where I usually kept it on the small stone table. In the darkness, I stumbled to the hearth where I found the remains of buried coal and some flint. Back at the table, I lit the lamp. Nothing appeared to be out of place, but my hearth was almost cold. Sweat beaded on my forehead. As I moved the lamp about to see, I noticed the extra pair of sandals I had thought to give Lemuel, but never done. I dreaded what I might see as I shone a light on the area where Ott and his wife usually slept.

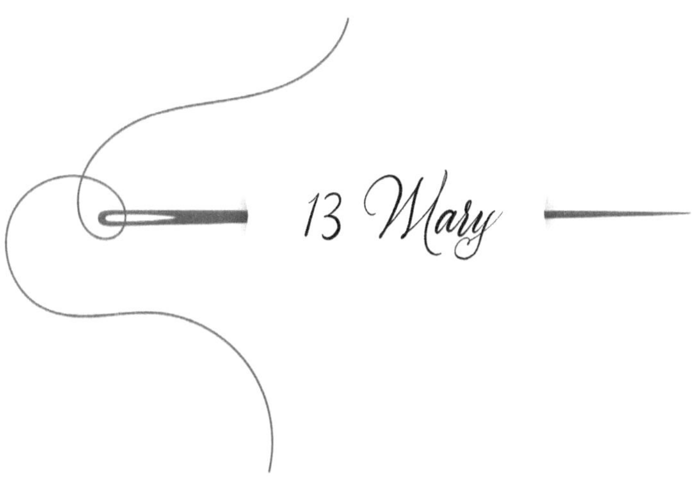

13 Mary

My child, do not let these escape from your sight; keep sound wisdom and prudence and they will be life for your soul and adornment for your neck.

Proverbs 3:21–22

The time came for me to spend the evening in Master Arthrimian's rooms the very next day. Sangie told me to prepare to meet with him and laid out the beautiful garments I should wear, giggled, and left. I was fearful and felt my skin go cold all over my body. I was contemplating how to get around the encounter when I hit upon an idea.

Grinning Sangie, with a vial of perfume in his hand, came back into the room, and I ducked my head, trying to look sad-faced. "I need your help," I said, lying. "My moon cycle has come. Please bring me some rags to sit on so I do not soil myself or anything."

He went quickly and came back with a mesh sack full of rags and a basin of water. "I am so sorry," he said. "Master will wait to see you until you have finished for the prescribed number of days and cleansed."

"Alright," I said. He left, and I lay on the bed hoping I had given myself some time to plan a successful escape. I prayed my lie would not cause me any problems.

I stayed in my room for three days, and continued to gaze at the green area I thought to be an oasis. If I made it there, where could I go? The sunrise and sunset gave me a general direction to travel. Food was amply delivered to my room. I stowed dried fruit, hard cheese, and bread, and kept a flask of watered wine hidden in the bed covering. I hid it all among the hanging garments before Myanna came to clean my room.

On the morning of the fourth day, Sangie came in with my breakfast, smiling and cheerful as always. I asked to go to the bath and cleanse myself, and he took me there. He brought me a vial of perfume.

"It is the master's favorite," he said.

As we were going back to my room, I heard a man's voice raised, commanding someone to do something. There were other voices, but I did not understand what was said. When I dismissed him, Sangie left me in my room to dress.

In a short while, I heard a horse-drawn carriage arrive. The clanging of the metal sound of a gate closing echoed in my window. I looked out, but could not see the front of the house I was in. As I gazed for a long time with nothing else to do, I saw a carriage trail of dust as it went toward the area where we had traveled coming here. I needed to find out how to get out of my soft prison, and wondered if Sangie would help me. Or dare I even tell him?

A while later, I saw Carabel in the courtyard, accompanied by two servant women. She wore a richly embroidered cream outer robe, and her hair was covered with a blue scarf. Blue was a rare expensive luxury as the dye came from many sea snails. I thought to call to Carabel but decided against it. She was a concubine of Master Arthrimian and being even more coddled. I did not want to be subjected to any advancements from him. My little lie had probably caused her to be with the master for more than one night. I felt sorry for her, but there was nothing I could do to help. Had Arthrimian left? I hoped he was gone.

Sangie came with a tray of food and some wine. I was growing accustomed to being fed, bathed, and having no work to do. It would be so easy to slip into such a routine, but I did not want what I feared went with such pampering. I might never see my brother and sister, Jesus, Uncle Elias, neighbor Simon, or any of our friends again.

"Sangie, may we explore the house and grounds? I want to see more of the rooms if I may." I was forming a plan, even though the request sounded innocent. He eyed me thoughtfully and did not answer immediately. "Is there a part of it you prefer to see?"

"I have wondered where the kitchen is located, and if there is an outside oven where bread is baked. Where I live, our oven is outside the house, and there is a hearth in the kitchen where we keep a fire and kettles for cooking."

"You will never be required to cook. It is much the same here, except perhaps on a larger scale. I see no harm in taking you there."

"Was it Master Arthrimian who left?"

"Yes, he will not see you until he returns in a few days." Upon hearing he was gone, I breathed a quiet sigh of relief.

When Sangie came to take me for a tour, he was jovial, almost excited to be escorting me around. "Down this hallway is Master Arthrimian's quarters, and next door to him is the unoccupied room for his favorite concubine. He is not yet married, but I have heard he is looking for an arrangement with a prominent family. Carabel's room is at the opposite end on the same level as you.

After walking the hallway, we descended a rather narrow stairway, rounded a corner, and there I beheld the kitchen. Two massive stone fireplaces adorned a wall, and steaming kettles hung there. Delicious aroma of stew filled the air. Two men and two women were handling dishes and cutting vegetables and what appeared to be lamb and birds. They nodded to us and continued to work. They all wore plain natural colored loose garments and had bare feet. I wondered how long they had been in service to Master Arthrimian.

"Hello," I said and smiled.

One of the women looked up at me and said, "Hello." She was probably Judean, or related to the Judeans, as she reminded me of Martha.

I wondered if she simply repeated what I said, or if she knew my language. I saw a door to the outside, and asked Sangie, "Is the oven out there?"

He led me out the door to see the two large ovens nestled in the earth. While I was out I beheld a problem in my plan. Past the ovens, the dry stream trench and embankment were deep and steep. There was a stench in the air of rotting food scraps and human excrement. We always buried our offal, so it took me aback. Rich people did not necessarily have clean habits. I supposed everything was dumped into the trench.

Once back inside, I noticed the kitchen was very

warm, and I wondered where they kept vegetables, meats, and wine before food was to be prepared. How many people lived in the house besides Master Arthrimian? Four of us had recently arrived, and I saw four in the kitchen. Neither of the women kitchen slaves was the one who had cleaned my room. There must be more people.

"Is there anything else you wish to see?"

"Have you a cellar for keeping vegetables?"

He giggled, nodded, and led me back out of the kitchen around a corner where there was a small door in the floor. He pointed to it but did not open it.

"Thank you," I said. I noticed a niche beside the cellar door entrance where servant garments hung on pegs. "We can go back now as I am tired," I said.

I thought about what I might do. If I could grab one of the servant garments from the peg, I could also braid my hair like Myanna, who had cleaned my room. I had a similar head covering in grey. Since we were near the same size, anyone who saw me would think I was her.

I had watched for people outside and noticed little or no movement in the time past the evening meal before it became dark. The moon had grown in the last few days and would be full soon. Dare I go out and climb the steep embankment of the dry stream? I began to think it was not a dry stream, but a ditch that had been dug to protect the master's large home. My next thought was where to go after I reached the distant oasis. I did not know anything about the trails, or where I was. I could only rely on my inner thoughts and my trust in YHWH. Jesus had said his father would always be with him and his followers. I dared to believe I was a Follower, even though I had not been called to be a disciple or diaconate. I heard him say to others, "Your faith has made you whole." If my faith was strong enough, perhaps it could sustain me. In my heart, I knew my brother was looking for me, and he had probably asked Jesus and his friends to search too. Neighbor Simon, who had always been kind to me, was a businessman who traveled. Perhaps he would know where to search and help look for me.

I did not leave, as I was fearful because I did not know where I would go. The next morning Sangie brought breakfast and was very cheerful. "What do you think of the fresh bread today? Is it especially good with the soft cheese spread on it?"

"It is delicious," I said, as I took a bite of it while he waited to see my appreciation. "The cheese is fresher than the last I had on bread, and it is indeed creamy. There is fresh fruit as I have never seen."

"Pomegranates and other fruits and cheeses were brought in by carriage the day Master Arthrimian left."

"Will the fruit be kept fresh in the cellar beneath the floor? I would like to see in there someday."

"We can go today after the kitchen is finished for the evening."

When we went, Sangie opened the cellar door. One had to grab the sides of the wall going down the steep seven stone steps to the earthy, cabbage-scented interior. Sangie shone a candle to reveal onions, turnips, and some other vegetables hung on the wall. He said, "Meats are inside crockery, salted or covered with herbal brines." Vegetables, herbs, and fruits were stacked on shelves. At one end of the room, there appeared to be a door, and I wondered if it went to the outside or yet to another chamber. "The small baskets hold dried spices which come from afar." We went back up the steps, and Sangie set the door to cover the entrance. "What did you think of it?"

"You have food stored to last a long time. I have never seen such a place. Does it have an outside entrance as well?"

"Yes, but it is too difficult to bring anything in. You have seen the large ditch." He giggled. "I am not sure whether much thought was given when it was built, unless they were planning to fill the trench with enough water to bring something in on small boats."

I laughed at his humor. I thought I would probably miss agreeable Sangie when I left. We strolled back to my room and on the way met Carabel with an attendant. "Hello, Carabel, are you doing alright?"

"Yes," she said, but bowed her head. From her reaction, I wondered if she would want to escape with me if we could. We both kept moving, so there was no time to talk. I wondered if we were purposefully kept separate so we could not plot an escape or other mischief.

We came to my room, and Sangie asked, "Is there anything else you need tonight?"

"My flask is almost empty."

He did not take the flask but left to bring me another. When I sipped, it was watered wine. "Thank you. May YHWH bless you."

He nodded, smiled, and waved as he left my room. When I looked out my window, I saw the moon gave glowing light. Either tonight or tomorrow night I knew I must take a chance and leave so I could take advantage of the moonlight to travel. I wanted to be gone before Arthrimian returned.

I braided my hair into one long plait. I put on a light tunic and tied a sack around my waist containing bread, dried fruits, cheese, and rags. The two flasks I also tied about my waist beneath a second tunic. I tied my grey head covering on. My life pulse beat loudly in my ears, and I was sure everyone in the building could hear it. The time for me to leave had come.

I waited until I heard no footsteps or any other movement in the house. I thought of Carabel but decided it was too dangerous to have both of us leave at once, especially since I had not been able to talk with her. Perhaps I could help someone find her later and rescue her. I opened my door slowly and peered out. It was clear. I went all the way to the kitchen, thinking I would leave by its back door. When I came to the place where servant clothing hung, I took one loose garment and slipped it on over my clothing. I eased open the door to the kitchen.

Startled, I was not alone. One of the men who had been cooking earlier was sitting and eating a round of bread and drinking from a goblet. He had his back to me, but if I went through there he would see me. He turned suddenly, sensing something. "Myanna, what are you doing here? I told you we must be careful until we know we can safely leave. We will find a way, and then we can begin a family."

Thankful the light was dim, I did not know how to answer. He thought I was the cleaning slave, Myanna. He spoke Aramaic with a few words in Canaanite. She had pretended not to know anything I said when I spoke with her, but perhaps she had understood. I bowed my head and turned to go. He did not follow. I felt bad for the pair who had likely been sold into slavery as I had been.

I went into the cellar, and stumbled, pulling the door as closed as possible behind me. Upright, in dank darkness, I felt my way to the back door of the cellar. When I tried to open it, I found it was either locked from the outside or stuck from not being used. I wondered how else I could leave. I went back up the steps thinking to lift the cellar door but halted when I heard footsteps. Now my skin prickled in fear. The kitchen man approached the cellar door.

I had ducked into the cellar, but couldn't budge the door to the outside. When I heard footsteps overhead,

I remained still as possible hidden in the darkness, sure my loudly thumping life pulse would give me away. The kitchen man descended steps quickly, then went to the back door of the cellar and did something to force it open. "Myanna, are you out there?"

I was relieved he still thought I was his woman, and not me. I wondered if he might even help me if I asked but thought it was too much of a risk. He stood, highlighted in the moonlight at the doorway, waiting. Fetid air seeped in. As he turned and came back into the cellar, he pulled the door closed. I had hoped he would leave it ajar.

I was too frightened to move from behind a large stone crock where I hid, even after he had ascended the stairs and closed the door behind him. I stayed until I heard no more footsteps. Since I had seen the backdoor open, I knew it was possible, so I decided to try again. I lifted the latch, then put my weight against it, but it did not move. What had the strong kitchen man done to open it? When I lifted the latch, I kept hold of it, and even though it took all my strength, moved it upward some more. It creaked open! Rocks and sticks littered the ground and some were in front of the door and made a crackling sound as I opened it. I couldn't breathe for a moment. I was frightened but knew I had no time to lose.

I quickly made sure all my provisions were attached to my waist beneath the servant tunic and shut the door. I hoped I had not made too much noise. I stood, looking at the embankment in front of me, engulfed in shadows. Where I stood, I would have to slide down and then climb up a steep bank with no handholds. I crept in the shadow of the house, looking for a better way. I tried sliding down, then scaling upward, but slid down as much as up. I scraped and soiled my hands as I crawled back up near the house. I heard a noise. Small eyes beaded at me, it was only a rat.

Abruptly, I was grabbed roughly from behind by a man with strong arms. He hoarsely whispered, "Where are you going, leaving without me?"

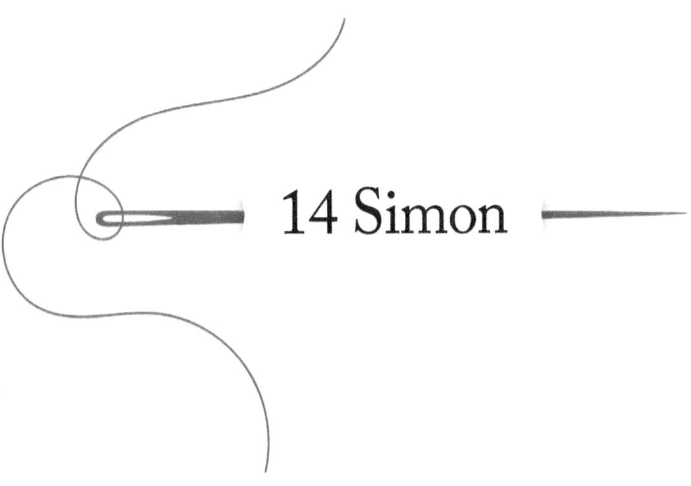

14 Simon

Two are better than one, because they have good reward for their toil. For if they fall, one will lift up the other; but woe to one who is alone and falls and does not have another to help.

Ecclesiastes 4: 9–10

A chilly emptiness engulfed me as I opened the door to my home. My manservant and his wife were not there. No parchment note had been left, as Ott could not have written one. Nothing appeared to have been thrown around as if there had been a thief. I looked inside food crocks and flour bins. Vials of olive oil sat on shelves, grain and flour were in bins, and wine was in the stone crockery. I found a round of creamy cheese, untouched, but only stale dry bread. Dates and figs were in a bowl on the table.

I was at such unease at my discovery which gave no answers, I almost forgot why I had come. I took a blanket from the corner where I had always slept on a soft bed. I poured a cup of wine and sipped it slowly. When I was finished, I filled two flasks with wine from the stone storage jar. Next, I took the hard bread, cheese, and a knife, and filled my waist pouch with dried fruit. While I wished for fresh bread, there was none. Being unclean, I could not implore my neighbors as to what happened, or to beg bread from Martha.

I secured my door and went back to the tomb area where my worn earth spot by the gnarled tree welcomed me. As I lay down on my blanket, I couldn't sleep. A night bird sounded and I heard the faint clopping and swishing wheels of a donkey cart being run on the trail which goes around the mount, not toward Jerusalem. It was the same sound I had heard on another night, shortly before I had heard from Lazarus his sister Mary had disappeared.

I had nothing else to do, so I scurried up from my blanket and made my way through the brush to find out if I could see anything. In the half light, I heard a man quietly commenting, "They are asleep from wine. I do not think they will give us any trouble."

Creeping as close as I dared, I listened, but no more conversation ensued. I wondered what they could be talking about unless they had some people inside the cart. I could not hope to be near anyone as I was unclean, so I grasped my bell to silence it. The cart wheels stopped. I stopped. I waited for what seemed to be a long time.

They were probably down for the night. When all was silent, I came closer and saw the cart, a donkey bedded down, and the forms of two men nearby lying down. I waited. Carefully, I crept closer to the cart. It was covered and tied. Possibly, it only held items to be traded somewhere. Dare I untie it and peer inside? I waited until I heard snoring from the men sleeping on the ground. Curiosity kept me there. When I was next to the cart, I heard anxious breathing. My life pulse quickened. Someone was inside, and I wondered who and why. I discounted the idea it could be Ott and his wife, as no struggle had been apparent in my house.

With a drumming pulse, I quietly untied the rope to the cart's cover, and carefully inched it open a little at a time. Two people were inside! I heard a quick intake of squeaky breath as a woman gasped. What could these men be doing with them? Were these their own women? Were they slavers? A chill ran down my back. Could this have happened to Mary? Should I help these people, or would I give them leprosy if I tried? I left the cover untied and rushed away so I could find someone. My legs quivered and threatened to make me stumble. I wondered who I could get to help. Would anyone listen to me?

I had very little energy but ran until I was panting like a running horse. I came to the courtyard by my house in Bethany. There was a lamp still burning in Martha's house. I knocked on the door and stepped back from it. When Lazarus answered, and saw it was me he came outside. I backed away. "Good evening."

"Good evening to you, and what brings you here at this hour all out of breath?"

"I believe there are slavers who have some people in a cart out on the mount's upper side trail. Please follow me, but not closely. I want to help them get free from the cart where they are kept."

"Are you sure? You are not imagining things in your state of physical illness and distress?"

"No, and Ott and his wife are not in my house. Do you know what happened to them?"

"I haven't seen them, but they do keep to themselves. Perhaps they are with his wife's parents. Let us go see if we need to help some people."

We hurried along, and I asked, "Has Mary come home?"

"No, and we have asked everyone we know, searched

everywhere she might have gone." Lazarus' voice was husky with sadness and frustration. "Jesus was here and left again. He had not seen her."

"I am so sorry. I have had her visit me in a dream. I hope she has not been killed."

Lazarus did not respond to me but hurried along behind me. We approached the trail where I had seen the men and the cart. I had removed my bell, and we both walked as quietly as possible. I pointed to the cart outline. Lazarus motioned to me to stay at a distance while he went to inspect the cart.

Soon I heard whispering and the sound of quick footsteps walking toward me. I knew I must back away, and I did. I whispered, "I am here, but I am unclean and cannot help up close." It was too dark to see who it was, only the outline of two women with Lazarus.

He came past me with the women. I was horrified to see in the moonlight one of them looked like Ott's wife, Naomi. The three hurried on ahead of me on the trail. I kept away from them so no one would have to see or smell my leprosy. I knew now what might have happened to Mary, and I was sick at heart. Could it have been the same night I had heard a donkey cart on the upper side mount trail? She was probably far away and subject to foreign men. How terrible!

"Please give my best to Ott and his wife."

"His wife Naomi and daughter Sarah are with me, but we need to hurry or those men will awake and pursue us."

"Thank you." I needed to speak with Lazarus soon, but not now. If Jesus could heal Lemuel, I wanted him to try to heal me too.

The next evening, I crept up to my house in the dark. I tried the door, and it was locked. I had a key hidden beneath a certain rock, and I used it. Once more, I discovered my house was cool. No hearth fire or lighted lamp, no cooking aromas met me. I had hoped Ott would at least be there. It occurred to me that perhaps too much time had elapsed, and I had not paid him. Would he have left me without a word? He had always been faithful as had his wife. Probably, the trauma of being kidnapped was too much for her, and they had gone to be with her parents temporarily. Had these same men stolen Mary?

There was a loud knock on my door. I was afraid to open it, lest the slavers were back to retrieve the women they had lost. The knock came more softly. "Simon, are you inside your house?"

I breathed a sigh of relief as it was the voice of Lazarus. I flung the door open and stepped far back into my room. "How are you and the family? What have you found out about these slavers?"

"Ott and I let the authorities know, and of course with the Romans and Sadducees, you never know how much help you will get. Jesus is supposed to come back from Galilee, and when he does, we are going to look for Mary. Word has it the slavers are selling their people in Egypt and sometimes Greek Isles. We can travel over land, or charter a boat and begin there."

"Will Jesus heal me?"

"Are you finally ready, my friend?"

"I will do anything he says, pay any price. I am so glad Ott's wife and daughter are safe."

"Ott has been so distraught since they were taken on their way to get water. He stayed with his wife's parents to help calm them."

"Thank you, Lazarus. Please let me know when Jesus comes."

We bid goodnight and he went home. I thought about staying in my house but decided I should not lest Ott and his family return. Despair washed over me again. Would any of this have happened if I had professed my faith as Lemuel had before Jesus healed him? I did not know, and I tried to say prayers I had been taught in the synagogue when I was a youth before my bar mitzvah. When I tried to pray now, it was as if I had blown a feather up into the air and it had not floated, but fell like a rock. Had I lost even my heritage, my connection to the God of Israel?

A thought, as from an unseen being, demanded my attention. Perhaps I had not been healed because I needed to be here to hear the cart and suspect foul play. Might YHWH have used me to save Ott's wife, Naomi, and their daughter?

I took wine, fruit, and cheese, locked my home, and slunk back to my place by the tombs beneath the gnarled old tree where my blanket awaited me.

Deep disappointment washed over me in waves like being caught on a shore in a storm surge. Alone, my hopes were dashed to pieces. I didn't tip the wine flask to my mouth but curled my dry lips in grievous inner hurt. Had YHWH truly used me, or could anyone have done what I did for Ott's family? Would I die tonight?

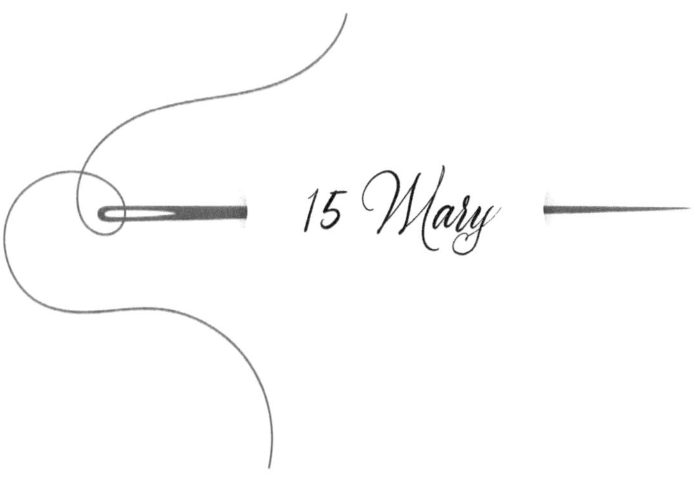

15 Mary

*But surely, God is my helper;
the Lord is the upholder of my life.*

Psalm 54:4

The kitchen worker was hurting me with his tight grip. I had no hope of getting away. I said, "I am Mary, not Myanna as you suppose." The man was strong, and I wondered how he truly felt about Myanna as his hold had me gasping for breath.

He released his grip a little but did not let me go. "Why are you dressed in Myanna's clothes, with your hair done like hers?"

"I was hoping to escape by pretending to be her until I was far away from this place."

"You must be one of the new concubines. How would it be if I reported you to Master Arthrimian?"

"Has he returned?"

"No, but he will." His voice was firm, threatening.

"You and Myanna plan to escape, why would you not help me? I am a slave as well as you."

He released his hold on me. "As one of his newest women, you are treated very well. Myanna saw the luxurious rooms and finery you women have been given. Why leave such a nice life where you can have anything you want?"

"It is not everything I want. I am homesick for my family, a long way from here, but I am determined to find my way home."

"Do you have a husband and children?"

"No, but I want a good life. I do not want to be a man's concubine slave and treated as his possession. I have a friend named Jesus, and I had hoped Uncle Elias would make arrangements so I could become his wife. He would come and help me if he knew what has happened. Perhaps you have heard of the teacher and his miracles?" I was very fearful and shaking, not knowing what the man would do. He released me.

"No." He was quiet for a long moment, then sighed and said, "Follow me, and I will show you the best way to climb out of here." We walked a little way, then down a short incline into the dry bed below. We kept going in the ditch until we were near the bridge at the front entrance. He showed me some stone planks to use as hand and foot holds as I ascended, a good place for me to climb up and out. It was probably a way used to repair the bridge supports. "No one is to know I helped you, or I could be thrown out or worse, lose my life. May good fortune follow you."

"May YHWH protect you. I will not speak to anyone about your help. Thank you so very much. I hope you and Myanna can leave soon. If I follow the trail, where will I be going?"

"One way, the road you recently came, you will return to the port city where you may find help. The other way will get you to an oasis and some trails or roads going a couple of directions. I am not sure where they lead a traveler."

"I thank you again. YHWH bless you with peace," I said. My hands were scratched and dirty going up the embankment beneath the bridge, but I could almost taste freedom.

"Go with El." He said softly and raised his hand and turned away.

In fear and trembling hands, I made my way up to the trail. It was not difficult, but my life pulse beat loudly.

At first, I ran in the direction of the port city where there were people who might help me, but something made me stop. Was it YHWH, or Jesus, or my own insight telling me to go the other way? I turned around and walked fast, deciding to preserve my strength. Nothing was in my path all night, and the bright moonlight seemed to direct my steps.

The day dawned gloriously on a lonesome barren terrain. The small green spot I thought to be an oasis I had seen from my room was not near. Hunger got the best of me, so I sat beside the trail on warm sand devoid of any plants. I opened a flask and sipped sparingly, not sure where the next liquid would come from, and I broke off a bite of bread to eat. Satisfied, I got up and walked on the trail in the endless sunshine, wondering how far until the green spot would appear. Surely it was there, as I had seen it from my window far off. Had I not been so elated to be free, I would have despaired at not knowing the way I should go. I went on, putting one foot in front of the other. Sometimes one has to keep going in spite of the circumstances. Faith in our benevolent YHWH carried me on. He had freed our ancestors from slavery in Egypt and eventually delivered them to a better life.

I wondered what Master Arthrimian would say, and how he would react when he returned and found I had disappeared. Would they send horsemen looking for me? Only the kitchen man knew I had left. What about Sangie? I would miss him. Would they question the entire household? While I kept walking, keeping the pace I had established, I realized the trail was now sloping downward. I was not hidden. Some brush and small trees began to appear ahead of me. The small rise on which Master Arthrimian lived was not nearly as tall as Mount Olive.

I felt a presence as I walked. Was it YHWH or Jesus, the man I loved? I did not meet anyone. Below me was the green oasis area I had longed to see up close. I was elated. I ran toward the green respite, even as it kept moving away from me. It was a mysterious happening. Once I was there, I saw a spring bubbling water from grey rocks. Exhausted, I sat and removed my sandals. Washing my feet and hands felt so good after my trek. Shade from some trees made me comfortably cool, and I rested and refreshed myself with food and watered wine from one almost empty flask. I dipped it into the spring and refilled it. I knew I should not get too comfortable here, lest someone come. I heard a noise that sounded like an animal lapping water. Was it a lion, or some other dangerous beast? I waited, afraid to look in the shadows. Whatever it was must have gone off after drinking its fill. Perhaps the beast feared me. I could not be sure. I wanted to remain vigilant, but my eyes would not stay open as I had walked all night and most of the day, and I drifted off to sleep.

When I awakened I could not believe I had slept so long. The sun was setting at the rim of the earth. I refastened my flask and started walking again. In truth, I did not know where I was going, but my destination was Bethany. I said all the prayers I knew, hoping they would be heard. "Hear, O Israel, the Lord our God, the Lord is One. Blessed be his Name." I felt a peace, thinking about his protection, hoping for his shield. What did Lazarus say? "Under the shelter of his wings." Were those wings keeping me safe? I trusted it.

Darkness and moonlight have a way of distorting images. I thought I saw someone in the distance on the trail. I wondered how it would be to catch up with another person, but worried it could be a bad person like the slavers who had captured me. I slowed my steps, contemplating the possibilities. It could be a good person, someone who would help me find my way home. How would I know unless I caught up with him? I would welcome a companion.

I was getting closer as I walked, and sped up, then slowed as I worried. Who else would be on the trail? What if it was Lazarus or Jesus, or even neighbor Simon looking for me? The night air had been crisp and cool but became still and damp. I felt the need to remove my cloak but had no place to put it, so I kept it on. I had gotten into the situation I was in by being too trusting of a stranger. I learned a lesson from the experience. I stopped walking, and waited, as I decided not to encounter the person. The individual did not move. I chuckled softly to myself and kept walking until I came up to the dry stump which had once been a lone tree. I had supposed it was a person in this treeless place. How many years ago had it been a live tree? I laughed, but I was not amused at my error which had unnerved me.

I felt lonely and was disappointed it had not been someone who could help me. I still did not know where I was going on the trail, whether it was the right direction, or if I would find help. The night air had become dense, and I knew a rain storm was probably looming. I heard a growling rumble coming from the dark cloud in the distance. Light streaked across the sky, thunder crashed loudly as more lightning flashed. My cloak became drenched, but I was alright, and I continued to walk in the cover of darkness. I welcomed the coolness. Some clouds remained, blotting the sun as day came and rain ceased. My feet grew weary as the day wore on, and I hoped I would find a town soon. I saw what appeared to be a low enclosure or buildings in the distance and hurried toward it. I stumbled and regained my footing, berating myself for giving in to aching in my whole being.

It was evening when I approached a short fence made of stone rubble that surrounded a small town. The narrow gateway was open. Men, with blue strips dangling from their wrists, wearing modestly decorated shawls, walked toward a building. A shofar sounded. Trilling children, cackling chickens, and assorted dogs wandered around. Women called to each other and to their children. They stopped to look at me curiously. I am sure it seemed strange for a young woman to come into town unaccompanied by a man or family, especially in this remote place. Doors shut as women gathered their children inside. No one spoke to me, and I was sorely vexed. Even though they appeared to be similar to the Judeans where I lived, they were not practicing traditional hospitality. Afraid no one would want to talk with me, I decided I must try to speak to someone who might show me the way toward Bethany. I knocked on the wood and metal door of a small sand brick house. A woman, dressed in a long tan tunic, opened the door a crack at first. "What do you want?" she asked in Canaanite and Aramaic.

"I am lost," I said, holding back tears at having someone speak to me in my own language. I could not tell by her demeanor if she would help me, let me in, or rebuff me. Her dark grey-streaked hair was revealed partially around the edges of her head covering. She appeared to be about Martha's age.

I stood waiting, tears trickling down my cheeks. The woman's stern demeanor changed when she saw my despair. "Come inside to sit and have some water." Her brown eyes were kind. A little boy in a soft tan tunic hid behind her. Two young girls in bright-colored garments sat on the floor rolling a ball of yarn back and forth between them. Savory cooking aromas filled the air.

"My name is Mary from Bethany. I was forcibly taken by some slave traders and sold to a Master Arthrimian who lives at least four days' walk from here. I escaped, and carried only two flasks and a small amount of food."

"I am Prisca. Your fine cloak is of Egyptian style, and I was untrusting of you. If no one else greeted you, they were fearful and thought you might be leading someone to harm us. Others probably thought you would not speak our language. We are near the borders, but still in Egypt."

I sipped water and supposed they had a spring or newly filled cistern as it tasted fresh. "I am so grateful to find a community of people who remind me of home. I want to go back to Bethany where I live, but I do not know how I will get there. I am sure it is rugged country, or possibly across some waters to go there. Do you know?"

"I will ask my husband, Jacob, when he comes from prayers. Someone will know how to help you, I am sure. Will you sup with us?"

"Thank you, yes. I heard the shofar and wondered if I have missed remembering a holiday." The wonderful smell of a vegetable and lamb stew had already enticed me and I was hungry.

"We are so far from other places. We celebrate small events with the shofar and prayers."

They only spoke of daily happenings after Jacob welcomed me to their low table. He had spoken privately with Prisca before we sat down, so she told him what she knew about me. The meal she made was a delicious stew along with vegetables and some barley bread. After prayers, I ate hungrily.

I helped Prisca clear the table and wash the dishes. She asked me about my family, and we shared as friends about cooking. "Martha must be a wonderful person," she said.

"I miss her so much and hope she and my brother are well. Have you ever heard about a man named Jesus?"

"Why do you ask?"

"He is an amazing man, a rabbi who has performed

miracles and speaks with wisdom. He has a group of followers who are learning from him. If I were a man like my brother Lazarus, I would be near him all the time as I adore him."

"Be careful loving such a man. A rabbi will be too much involved with other people to give his wife and family attention." Prisca wiped her hands on a rag and called to her four children who had run outside after the meal. "Children, come inside now. Anna do not dawdle." She put her children to bed, and Jacob was outside the house. I sat, with too much on my mind to sleep, wondering if anyone in this small settlement would be able to help me. Would Jesus come help me? It was probably too much to ask YHWH because he had the whole world to look after.

Prisca said, "We seldom have guests, as you probably could tell by Jacob and our shy children's reluctance to even ask you questions. I was barren for a few years after my marriage to Jacob, but one day I began to be with child and as you see I have four healthy ones."

"I am happy for you being able to bear children. It is a gift from the Lord. I do not know what is next, but I trust YHWH to help me."

"You may stay here tonight. We will talk in the morning about how to help you."

"I wish I knew how far away I am from home."

She simply shook her head as she did not know. She put a blanket of tan woven wool on the floor in a corner of the room and went to tend a child who was calling for her. While I was not near Bethany and did not know how far away it was, I fell asleep, dreaming of Jesus coming to rescue me, and feeling safe for the first time in a long while. It was as if a benevolent presence surrounded me.

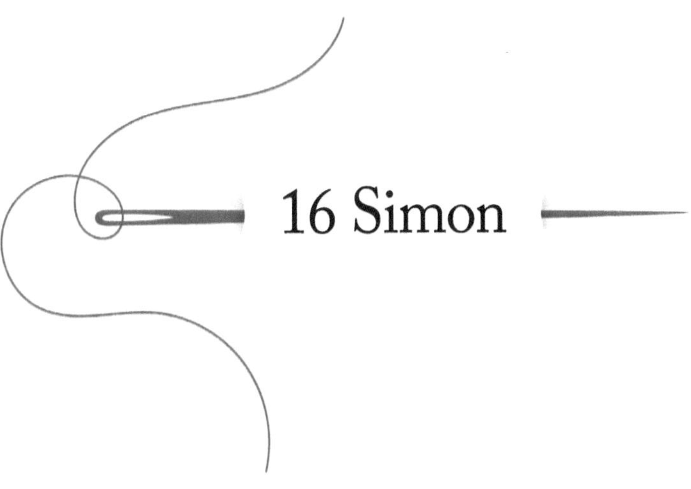

16 Simon

Better is the end of a thing than its beginning; the patient in spirit are better than the proud in spirit.

Ecclesiastes 7:8

I awakened during the night, feeling miserable within my leprous body and spirit. In the moonlight, my aching hands were white and leprous, my fingers and especially fingertips numb. Could there be any hope? Would I die without ever having another opportunity to be healed by Jesus and no possibility to marry and leave a son? How could I pray without proper tefillin or a prayer shawl here? What should I pray for if I could? I was thinking only of myself and found no answers. Sounds of night prowling animals caused my neck and left arm skin to erupt in many prickles as if entangled in a briar patch.

After waking from a fitful sleep, I heard the stonecutters talking and making noises with their implements. It was the tomb I had contracted them to construct for a wealthy family, not for me. At the time, I had no need of one for many years. I looked at my hands which had been white as limestone in the middle of the night. They were still colorless in daylight and my fingers devoid of feeling, except endless prickling in a couple of them.

I hoped Ott and Naomi and their daughter Sarah were once more in my home and secure from harm. They had gone to be with her parents after the women were safe and returned. I should find a way to get money to Ott, as I was overdue to pay him. I listened attentively to sounds on the trail from Jerusalem up to Bethany. Surely Jesus would come again soon to see my neighbors and help them find Mary. I ached for the family as Lazarus and his sisters were very close, like a weaving. I knew many travel routes because of my business dealings. If only Jesus would heal me as he had done Lemuel, I could help search for Mary. I heard men coming up the Mount Olive trail, and I thought I heard Jesus's voice ring out with a psalm chant. I stood up and hoarsely called out, "Jesus, it is Simon, up here above the tombs. Please, if you will, heal me."

I listened. There was no response, so I cleared my dry throat and tried with my weak voice to call more loudly. "Jesus, I am ready to be healed. I will pay any price you ask." It came out squeaky and gravely.

There was still no answer, only muffled voices of men and their shuffling footsteps on the rocky trail. I sat down in defeat. I feared I had lost my opportunity when Lemuel had been healed. What had been the magic? How had it happened? I had seen scales drop from my friend's face as he had professed his faith. I rebuked myself for not having enough faith then to accept the offer to be healed. I questioned myself even now. Was I good enough to be healed? Had I done something in my youth to offend YHWH and was being punished? It was surely a failure on my part, but I could not remember what it was, or when it had happened. Faithless man, I berated myself, you do not even deserve to ask for healing. I judged myself to not be good enough.

In bright midday, I tilted the flask to my lips and drank deeply of the wine to soothe my throat. It was my only solace now. Even though I knew he was beyond where he could hear, I called in a hoarse voice for the third time today, "Jesus, can you hear me? Use your magical power. You healed Lemuel, and I ask you to heal me. I will pay whatever price you name, do anything you want me to do."

There was no answer. Having nothing to do but think, I tried to grasp what I might have missed. Lemuel had given nothing and he was healed. While it seemed impossible in my business experience, perhaps what Jesus offered to us was graciously and freely given. How could that be? I smiled at the possibility I had discerned a truth.

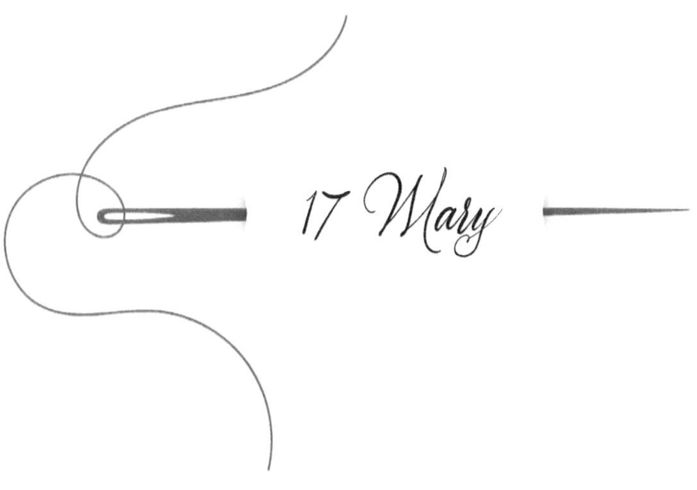

17 Mary

The angel of the Lord encamps around those
who fear him, and he delivers them.

Psalm 34:7

My feet had recovered mostly from the walk I had taken to be in this town, among these gracious people. I helped Prisca with dishes in the morning after a hearty breakfast of goat milk, boiled barley, and figs. I sat on the floor with Anna and Elizabeth and rolled the ball of yarn to them amid squeals of laughter. I was comfortable, like being at home, but I could not stay. I stood, and the smallest girl, Anna, tugged at my hand begging me to play some more.

"I want to be on my way," I said. I stroked her silky, light brown hair and thought how sweet it would be to have a child of my own.

"I understand your wish to be back with your family, yet I'm fearful of you being alone on a trail where you could be in all kinds of danger from beasts, men, or a sudden storm. Please stay. You are good company for me and have helped with the children."

The very scent of other humans, clean washed dishes, and lingering cooking aromas gave solace to me. I thought of what she said, and was sorely tempted to remain with these good people in the town, but I wanted very much to be back in my sister's home. "I have faith YHWH will be with me wherever I go. He has protected me all this way, and I know he will continue."

"Faith is a good thing, yet where was YHWH when you were taken by the slavers?"

"Had I not been taken afar, I would not have met you and your family." It was the only answer for her. I knew an abiding presence had been there for me during the trying times I had endured and had helped me escape with my young womanhood intact.

She nodded thoughtfully. "If you wait awhile longer, the men will go to Jerusalem to the Temple. You would be protected by my husband Jacob."

"How many days until the men will leave?"

"It will be after they have gleaned the crops. They will bring their offerings of thanks to the altar in Jerusalem. It will be Festival of the Weeks."

"Forgive me, but I do not want to wait so long."

"As you will." Prisca scurried around her house cleaning and tending the children. Except for common pleasantries, she said no more to me.

She packed a cloth sack with cheese, bread, dried fruit, and some root vegetables. We filled my flasks with water. "Thank you, I am so blessed to have stayed with your family."

Jacob said, "Once you cross a big stream you will be out of Egypt. If you do not tarry on the way, Jerusalem is about fourteen or fifteen sunsets walk from there. I pray you will be safe. Stay here and try to send word home is my admonition. Maybe your brother or his friend Jesus can come get you. I wish I had time to take you, but I have work to do here. May YHWH keep you in his care."

In the morning, Prisca and Jacob bid me a good journey going forward. The family and I repeated the Shema together, "The Lord our God, the Lord is one." The children waved, and I waved back until I was out of sight.

I was momentarily bereft, wishing I had the courage to ask someone to accompany me all the way home. As I walked on the worn trail beside the houses and outside the gates of the town, I thought about Martha and Lazarus and wondered where they were looking for me. A cold prickly feeling seeped into my bones. I felt very sad because I did not know and was sure they were grieved.

In the sandy deserted distance behind me, I saw what appeared to be a man leading a donkey laden with goods. I slowed my pace. As he neared the town gate, I could tell it was an older man who wore a turban, and his donkey had rugs rolled and tied onto its back. He looked familiar. When he came close, he greeted me, "YHWH's good day to you, young woman."

"YHWH's good day to you as well." He was old. I hesistated speaking with a man, but remembering him encouraged me. "Where are you coming from?"

"Oh, I come from many places. I am known as Zeke the Rug Man."

"I saw you before at a large gathering of people who were listening to Jesus. I am Mary from Bethany. Good to see you." I turned away, reluctant to engage deeply in conversation. I was hopeful I could trust him. Dust settled as his donkey stopped shuffling on the trail. The little donkey licked his nostrils.

"What are you doing so far from home? I meet many people, forgive me for not recognizing you. The teachings of Jesus are wise. I am glad you have heard him. Can I interest you in anything I have here? A nice pair of sandals?"

"I'm sorry, I cannot buy anything today." I shook my head. "As to why I am far from Bethany, it is a long story."

He nodded thoughtfully. "I need to be moving on, as I am traveling to Jerusalem." He patted his donkey, and the donkey huffed appreciatively.

My ears perked at his words, even though I had walked a short way ahead. I turned back to him. Now was not a time to be shy. "Zeke the Rug Man, I suppose you were going to stop at the town whose gates are here, but I need to go home to Bethany. Would you mind if I were to walk with you to Jerusalem when you go?"

"My travels are often lonely. I would very much like for you to walk with me, young woman." He did not stop at the town, only briefly at a well for water, and we walked on together. "How did you end up so far from home, Mary?"

"I was taken by slavers when I went for water, and they sold me to a man in Egypt. I escaped, and believe YHWH is helping me find my way home. I will say more later." I had a lump in my throat and could not talk. We kept pace with the donkey. A slight breeze felt welcome to my sun-kissed face, and it was peaceful as if the Lord traveled with us. Only the plodding sound of hooves and footsteps echoed. The scent of his donkey and trail dust filled my nostrils.

I decided to break the silence and find out a little

more about Zeke the Rug Man. "If I may ask, how did you become a seller of wares, walking everywhere?"

"It came about naturally. My people traveled to many lands as they were from the Nomadic Nabateans. My father's father and his father had traveled from afar and traded in spices, frankincense, and myrrh. Father sold skins, precious metals, burial spices, and traded all manner of goods with people. After they were gone, I heeded their advice and practices, and for many years have continued on my own walking to many places and trading. You might say I am going about doing my father's business."

"Your people must lead an interesting life. I suppose it was long ago. Lazarus told me a little about a group who lived somewhere in the area, I don't recall where he said. But I think he called them Nabateans. They were beset by conflicts."

He nodded. And I sensed he wanted to be quiet, so I entertained my own thoughts, wondering about my family. Would Martha be wringing her hands, worrying, and Lazarus angry with himself for not protecting me? "Do you have a wife?" I broke the silence and hoped I had not asked something he would rather not answer.

"No." He spoke quietly, and his face was guarded against emotion.

"Oh, I am sad for you." I was ashamed I had been bold.

He nodded and looked off in the distance, deep in thought. I was at a loss for the right words, not knowing if it was a death or other reason he had no wife and family.

"You are one who listens, Mary. It is a good thing."

"I have been told I am a good listener. I suppose it is a gift from YHWH. You must have many adventures as you travel."

"Yes, once I was beset by a band of robbers who took my donkey with all the wares. I did not put up a good fight and had to let go of Chavah, my sweet gray donkey. They hurried away with everything and left me with a bruised arm and a shattered spirit. I walked on, feeling dejected, but glad I had hidden money inside my garment. I could at least buy another donkey and perhaps a couple of items to trade to begin again. It was very warm, the middle of summer. My flask was empty by the time I came to an oasis. I filled it and sat to rest. It was nightfall and I dozed. I awakened with a start as a wet muzzle nudged my neck and shoulder. It was my donkey."

"Oh, what a wonderful reunion!"

"Not only Chavah, but very little had been removed from her back. I don't know how she escaped her captors. It was miraculous."

"What an interesting story. If only Chavah could speak!"

"It was years ago, and I have a different donkey now."

"Have you given him a name?"

"Shnek," Zeke said.

His donkey turned to look at us at the sound of his name. We both laughed. "He responds to his name. I hope and pray we have uneventful travels."

My feet ached from walking all day. The sun had become relentless, and no clouds decorated the blue heavens. Night would come soon. Mercifully, we moved beside a stream until he found a place shallow enough to cross. He announced triumphantly, "This is not yet the Nile, but we are almost out of Egypt, and if all goes well, in a little more than fourteen sunsets, we will be in Jerusalem!"

I was surprised and joyful and clapped my hands. He chuckled at my enthusiasm.

"My sister is a good hostess and as a diaconate, she serves the followers of Jesus and many other people in her home. When we get back to Jerusalem, and I to Bethany, I want you to come to our house and sup," I said.

"Right now, I am a weary old man and would like to stop beneath those sparse trees for the night. "

"I am also tired." I sat in welcoming coolness on the ground beneath a palm tree, whose pointed leaves had begun to have a hint of brown.

Zeke unrolled a rug. "I hope my accommodations will suit you, Mary."

"More than I could have imagined, Zeke, thank you." I smiled at his graciousness and good humor. We sat on rugs and shared food we had both brought along. It was a pleasant meal of dried fruit, cheese, and bread, and I was blessed to be with someone with whom I could sit and visit. I felt mostly safe.

"Do you know the tree we are sitting beneath?"

"No, I am not familiar with tree names."

"It is a date, and rare for it to grow right here, so we are fortunate to find such a tree. When near a water supply, one might find fig or some other fruit tree." He sipped wine from a flask, then laid back with his hands clasped behind his head. "If you would like, please finish telling me of your unfortunate encounter with slavers as you began earlier."

"I am too tired now." Once I smoothed my brown rug, I lay down and closed my eyes to sleep. Suddenly, I was rudely awakened by the ground beneath me pulsing with hoof sounds.

A man who was on a black horse rode full speed up to us. Zeke stood. The man alit, and in a gruff voice, began to ask Zeke questions. "What are you doing with this woman?" Turning to me he said, "Are you a sister of Lazarus of Bethany?"

"Yes, and what is it to you?"

He grabbed Zeke roughly and pinned his arms.

Fearful and indignant, I screamed, "Please do not hurt him, as he is helping me go home."

"Do not be so trusting, Mary. You have gotten yourself into trouble before." He wrestled poor Zeke to the ground.

Zeke struggled beneath the strong man's weight. I was terrified of the brute who held my benefactor on the ground and did not know what to do to help Zeke. I rushed over flung myself as hard as I could and grabbed the man's arm as it was pinning Zeke's neck. His arm was hard like the solid crockery of our large kettle, and I was helpless to make any difference. I pummeled him with my fists until he lifted his arm from Zeke's neck. He gripped my arm.

"Stop" I screamed. "You are hurting me, and you said you came to help me. If you wish to help, go away and let me return home with the nice rug seller who is accompanying me to Jerusalem and Bethany." My voice came out in gasps of fear and rage. Clouds formed and made a distant rumbling on the horizon and the air became dense.

He briefly let go of Zeke but held my arm firmly. "I heard you were a wild one, Mary. My name is Reuben, and your uncle Elias knows I came to look for you. I trust he will pay me richly for finding you."

"You do not deserve money. I do not know you, and I do not trust you as much as I do the rug man. Let go of me." The skies darkened with grey billowing clouds. I struggled against Reuben's grip on my arm, and when I did, he gathered my other wrist in his large hand. I did not know how I would get away from my captor. He kept a booted foot on Zeke's back.

With his full attention on me and the threatening skies, Reuben unintentionally released his boot hold on Zeke.

Zeke calmly sat, and said, "Shnek, come." The

donkey came quickly, and he commanded, "Get!" Shnek reared up and bumped my assailant's back with its front hooves. Caught off guard, Reuben fell forward, releasing my arms. I stumbled and recovered, avoiding being pinned beneath him. He swore, and rubbed at his eyes, as sand flew into them. His horse snorted but did not come to help his master.

Wind began to gust hard against me, but I ran as fast as I could down the trail. I knew the man could overtake me on his horse. Zeke was on his donkey in an instant, following me. With surprising strength, Zeke lifted me onto the donkey's back with him. It was then I realized the rugs and wares had been dumped where we had the struggle. Horse hooves pounded behind us. Light streaked, thunder clapped, lightning flared, and sand pelted us relentlessly, making it difficult to see. I kept telling myself to have faith. It was reassuring to know the sand and wind also kept Reuben from seeing well.

We were off the trail, going as fast as we could when we came to a cliff above a deep wadi. At the edge were brambles that scraped my leg when we began descending on a damp, but powdery animal path. I looked up to see the horseman stopped at the top of the canyon silhouetted like a sand statue against a flash of lightning. We hid beneath a rock outcropping. Neither of us spoke. Reuben moved around on the ridge, and I worried he would find our trail and hiding place. Wind roared and lifted the sand into the sky, dimming vision.

Thunder growled an ominous warning. Nearby lightning crackled and filled me with more fear.

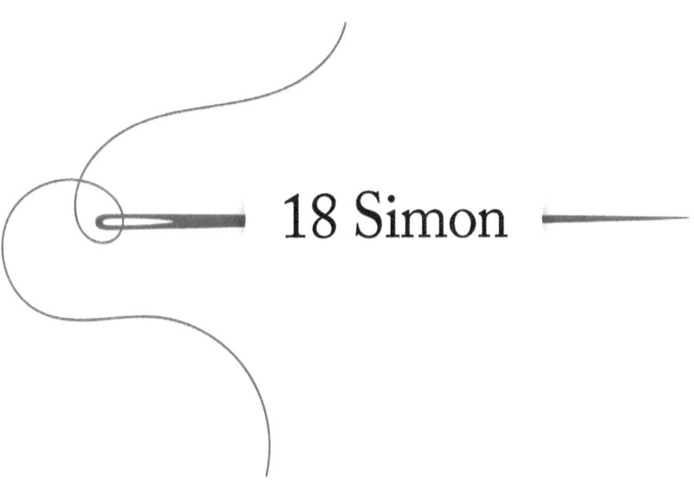

18 Simon

The righteous cry out, and the Lord hears them;
he delivers them from all their troubles.

Psalm 34:17

The sunlight shone on my face, and I lamented not feeling the fullness of joy I had in past times. I was unsure if it was real, as I heard the voice of Jesus saying, "Rise, Simon, I heard you call me."

I wondered if I was dreaming. I stood up and looked all around me, but saw no one. "Where are you, Jesus?" My dry voice cracked. I kept staring into the low brush behind me. He sounded too near to be on the trail.

"Simon, you called me."

"I did call. If it pleases you, I want to be healed of leprosy as you did for Lemuel. I have known you since you were a boy, but I know you have become a wise healer. Is there anything I need to do, any payment, to be well again?"

"You have done much, Simon. Yet you lack the most important thing."

Was it real? I was mortified. Now what did I need to do? "What is it? I can pay you whatever you ask. I have a home and some money saved as well. You may have it all if you will heal me. I will buy and sacrifice lambs. Please tell me."

"Do you remember the day your friend Lemuel was healed?"

"Yes, I remember it well. I have chastised myself ever since for not answering you immediately."

"What was it Lemuel gave in order to be made well?"

"He had to go wash and cleanse himself, and give a money gift at the Temple, I think. I do not remember you requiring anything else."

"Hmm. There was nothing else?"

He sounded like a typical rabbi, posing a question. "Not as I recall, Rabbi Jesus. I am miserable. Respectfully, why must I answer these questions? I do not remember Lemuel being tested like I am being examined." I tried to sound respectful even though he was younger than me by almost a decade.

"No, he answered rightly when I first asked if you and he wanted to be healed."

"Jesus, I know you well and have seen you and your followers in the home of Martha, Lazarus, and Mary. Please stop tormenting me. Have I not suffered humiliation and anguish enough with being an outcast, losing the chance to marry, losing out on many business opportunities, and not to mention my cursed physical appearance and pain?" I rapidly lost my patience. Acidic burning raged in my throat and stomach. I rasped, "Would you not agree YHWH has been unkind to me?"

"You have suffered, Simon, which is why I am here. Where is your faith?"

"Faith? I suppose leprosy has robbed me of it. How am I supposed to have faith in YHWH when I have been unfairly subjected to such a life as I am now living here among the tombs? Tell me." The air around me was like a thick fog, and I found it hard to breathe. I waited but received no answer. I still did not see Jesus. Perhaps this was another one of my strange dreams. After pausing, and more waiting, I asked, "Are you going to heal me or not?" I threw myself on the ground, grabbed at my clothing, and ripped off a sleeve, grieving. I reprimanded myself for my impatience with Jesus. I remembered the story my father told of how an ancestor Jacob had wrestled with God. But Jesus was not a god like YHWH. Was he?

I lay in the dirt and dust by the gnarled old tree which had become my home away from my home. Limestone dust permeated my nostrils, burning and almost strangling me. I listened to the craftsmen creating the tomb below. Someone was chanting songs. It grated in my ears to hear anyone being cheerful. I wondered where Jesus had gone when he had spoken yesterday. He had said I lacked something. If I could come up with the reason, I would be able to answer him rightly and be healed. Unless he had chosen not to heal me for a reason I could not comprehend. I had offered to pay any price! If healing was free, why hadn't he already made me well? Ott came with the basket in the evening, and I struggled down to get it, sliding most of the way. I called out, "Ott, thank you for bringing me sustenance. Are you back in my house, and is your family well?"

"We are back, and we are all well and thankful. I can never repay you and Lazarus for helping Naomi and our daughter Sara escape the slavers. Is there anything else I can do for you? Do you need clothing or another blanket?"

"My filthy clothing is enough for now as I cannot go anywhere. I owe you money, but I cannot access my funds in this condition. I want Jesus to heal me like he did Lemuel, but he refuses to do so, telling me I lack something. I offered to pay him whatever he wants, but he has yet to tell me what it is. I don't know what to do."

"Forgive me, for I am not a learned man, and what I say does not mean I think I know more than my master. Do you believe he can heal you? Do you have faith in him, and his ability to heal? Perhaps he wants to hear you say it plainly. When next you speak with him, if you get a chance to do so, let him know you believe he is sent from YHWH and you have faith he has the power to heal you."

"Ott, you are a good man and faithful servant for saying those words to me. I suppose I could say plainly I have faith. I told him I had lost my faith. You are suggesting I regain faith, and my faith will be the one thing I have needed to be well again." I tried to comprehend what he said. No money payment, only my faith would cause Jesus to heal? Did Ott believe Jesus was sent from YHWH?

"It is worth a try, forgive me, Master, but I suppose faith must be genuine, not some magical thing you try in order to be healed."

"Ott you are a faithful servant. Thank you for all you are doing for me without being paid."

"You saved my wife and daughter Sara by your quick thinking. My wife's parents thank you too. My family appreciates living in your home, and I am indebted to you. I must be on my way, so have a good night, Master Simon."

I thought for a long while about what Ott said to me. He was my servant, and I, his master. I was humbling my intellect to his. How could he know what I should do?

Nevertheless, I wanted desperately to be healed and back to doing my business. How could I gain faith I had lost after all the time as an outcast because of my leprosy? Some parts of my body ached and itched and many other parts had no feeling. I put my hand to my stomach to scratch but withdrew it instantly. Scratching always made it worse, and with a lack of feeling in my fingertips, I couldn't tell how deeply my fingernails dug into my skin until I drew blood. A cool breeze wafted about me suddenly.

"YHWH, thank you for the relief. My prayer was heard." I marveled at the sweet echo from a bird in the gnarled tree. "Jesus, if you are anywhere near, please give heed to my earnest plea to be healed. I believe in YHWH with all my heart. He created everything and is the Lord of our people from ancient times. You were sent from him. I trust in your ability to cure me of my terrible leprosy. You healed Lemuel, and I know you can make me well if you will. I want to have faith. Help me to have enough faith." My plea seemed weak and futile as Jesus was nowhere near.

I listened, but no answer came. I decided to wait patiently and lay my head down to rest on my blanket on the ground. I whispered, "I have faith you can heal me of leprosy, Jesus, even if you cannot hear me now, or come near to touch me. Next time you are passing near me, I will try to have enough faith. Even my business and my lost opportunity to wed are not as important as my being well again. It is all in your hands." I was amused at my quiet plea as Jesus was long gone from the mount. My eyes were weary, and I was dejected. I chastised myself for being too stubborn to turn my life back to true faithfulness. I had not done so soon enough. I thought of my idle mumbling to Jesus even though he was not in the area. I wondered if I had lost my senses.

I thought of little Mary, my neighbor, who was still missing last I had heard. I prayed she was alive and had not lost her faith. I fell asleep, vowing to help Lazarus find her whenever I became well again.

A raucous bird call awakened me in the early morning. I was hungry and reached into the basket for bread to break and eat. Dampness from dewfall cooled and eased my face. I put my hand up to wipe away the moisture, and when I looked at my hand I let out a squeal of joy like a young boy. "My hand is not white and scabbed! My sense of touch is back. My face does not feel numb or burn." I leapt up and danced around in the small space, being careful not to fall down the slope. "My body is cured." Could I trust this was not a dream?

I ran down to the tombs to see the men coming to work. "I am well. Jesus was not even nearby. He healed me. You men must have faith also. Jesus healed me!" As I whirled around my ragged robe flared exposing my legs. I jumped up and down like a child, laughing. "Faith, have faith in YHWH."

The men skirted around, avoiding any contact with me. I heard one exclaim, "The man has lost his senses. Master Simon has gone mad."

"Not mad at all, but healed by Jesus!" I said.

"I am healed, Ott," I exclaimed. I flung open the door of my house without knocking. My excitement at the healing of my body was too big to contain. I burst into uncontrollable laughter and was certain Ott would think I had lost my mind. "Healed of leprosy. I am well again and came back to the land of the living. I am not a cursed leper anymore. I can visit with people again. I can conduct business. I am healed!"

Ott rose from where he was seated with Naomi and daughter eating breakfast. "Master, it is good to see you. Oh, yes, I see your face is clear, and your hands are ruddy once again. What wonderful news. How did it come about?"

"Thank you for your wise advice about faith. I believe Jesus healed me, but I do not know how. I must bathe and put on clean garments, and go to the Temple with a thank offering. He did not tell me to do anything. I did not even see him, so I do not know by what means he performed the cure. I believe in him and his healing powers, the gift given to him by YHWH. He is truly a miracle worker, maybe even born of God himself." I clapped my hands like a child and marveled at the feeling of it.

"Shall I go with you to the pool to cleanse yourself? Or will you use your mikveh? I will bring fresh clothing for you to dress afterwards."

I sat on a mat on the floor. "Finish your meal with your family first. I will take a proper bath, and then do my purification in my mikveh. I would like to have you come with me to Jerusalem to pay my Temple dues and more. I fear my excitement will cause people to think I have gone mad."

I washed, and as I did, I examined my whole body. No lesions lingered anywhere on my skin. On our way to Jerusalem, I almost cried out loudly in joy but did not want to call so much attention to myself. My whole body felt clean and incredibly good. Sensation had gradually returned to all my fingertips. I had never felt so well.

Ott bid me a good day. I went to the Temple and put a good sum of my saved money into the treasury box. I looked up at the blue heavens and thanked YHWH again and again. Cleansed, dressed in my best tan tunic and cloak, I felt whole and blessed. I hoped to find Jesus and thank him.

Lazarus came striding toward me with a smile on his face. "Simon, I heard the good news. Jesus healed you. Martha wants you to come sup with us. It has been such a long time since your illness prevented us from being neighborly.

"Has Mary been found?" I asked as we grasped each other's shoulders as was our custom. A cloud seemed to settle over his face.

"No. Many have looked. Some leads have been followed. I think she is lost to us. We fear slavers took her and put her on a voyage across the sea."

"Little Mary has been heavy on my mind all the time I have had to think while I was alone and ill. I want to join in the search for her. Jesus must have cured me for a reason. I no longer have the urge to make more and more money to impress people. I will settle some business affairs here and be off to look for her. I don't know where to begin, but I have faith YHWH will show me the way."

"Thank you, Simon. We must go together if you want to search for her, but we have almost run out of places to look. A voyage across the sea can be costly and fraught with peril." His voice caught, near tears of frustration.

I saw his pain and realized we had both been suffering from different situations. Lazarus was grieved over the loss of a beloved little sister, and I had been pained with being a leprous outcast. Now healed, I hoped to be of more service than being merely a successful businessman.

"Will Judith's parents now restore your status as a future son-in-law?"

"No. I released them and her of all obligations to marry me when I had leprosy. As a peace offering, I told her father to keep the partial bride's price I had paid. By now, she probably has a new espousal pledge. I am sorry but I must think of it as something in the past. Later, I may pursue another bride."

Lazarus clapped me on the shoulder acknowledging our long-time friendship. "I thank YHWH again for your healing, my friend. How soon do you want to look for Mary? We will seek her. I think Jesus looked for her when he went to Galilee and other places. He comforted Martha and me. I trust he believes she is well. Since you do business in faraway places, perhaps we have a better opportunity to follow information people have given us."

"I will do it — rather we will. First, I have business to

attend to which I have neglected. We can leave then. I will hire a horse-drawn carriage to take us on the trail toward Egypt. It may be one way to follow her, even if she was taken across the sea. She could be in Egypt. If we cannot locate her there, perhaps we will go across the sea to look."

"I will let you take the lead on it, Simon. Look, here comes Jesus and his followers now. He has been away in Capernaum." Lazarus walked quickly toward the group and joined with many others who crowded around Jesus. Even though I desired to thank him, I held back, not wanting to intrude and call attention to myself. They turned and came in my direction, and I could not move, as I was hemmed in. His voice rang out, "Simon, are you well?"

I bowed low to the stone walkway, my head touching it. "Yes, Jesus, thank you in the good graces of our Lord for healing me. I cannot thank you enough. What must I do now?"

"Your faith made you well. You have done everything you needed to do. Go in peace. Serve YHWH, my father, show kindness to people, and listen to my instruction. Follow me."

"How shall I follow you when I have a business to run? I want to find Mary, sister of Lazarus, and plan to devote myself to searching for her until she is found. What must I do?"

He lifted his hand as a sign of blessing, looked at me, and then away. He was teaching those who listened to his every word but said no more to me. I walked home, pondering Jesus's admonition to follow him, and I did not know how I would do it. I had faith I would be shown the way. The faith gave me a deep inner peace like I had never experienced. I had grown a successful business in my youth and thought it was the way a man should go, and all he needed to do. My plan had been to have a home, wife, and family and leave heirs to continue my business when I would be gone. Now I sensed a new purpose, one of God's choosing for me. Not sure what it would be, I believed it could be an adventure. My thoughts filled with wild imaginings, and I had a fearful premonition.

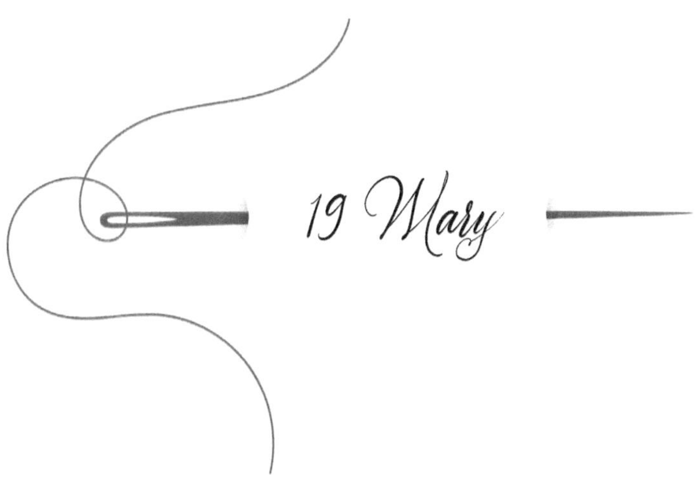

19 Mary

For he will command his angels concerning you
to guard you in all your ways.

Psalm 91:11

I was alternately too warm and my feet too cold as we waited, hidden, making no sound. Shnek was quiet, not even huffing. I wondered if Reuben was still above, watching for us to emerge. Rain came down in sprinkling waves with gusts of wind and pelting sand, but we were protected by the rock outcropping.

While the storm was making noise, Zeke whispered to me, "Are you doing alright?"

"Yes, I believe YHWH is watching over us." My arm and wrist felt sore where Reuben had clamped it in his strong hand earlier, but I did not complain. "What about the rugs and other wares?"

"We will not concern ourselves with those things right now, but be vigilant to keep ourselves safe."

As suddenly as it had come upon us, the sand storm blew away and left grit covering everything. Zeke peered out from the rock and shook his head. I wanted to ask but dared not since all was quiet. An animal skittered below us, making a noise almost like a newborn baby. Perhaps it was a small hyrax. I had heard of them before but had never seen one.

"Be still." Zeke put a finger up indicating I should stay with Shnek, and he slowly disengaged himself from our hiding place. He crawled down into the ravine. At a short distance from me, he came to a steep place and rolled down, then lay very still. I wondered why he had done so and was afraid he was hurt. I stood anxiously waiting for whatever was next.

Shnek shifted from hoof to hoof, as if wanting to

follow his master but stayed quietly with me. I listened for Reuben or his horse but did not hear anything. Zeke was completely still down below, and I feared for his life. I was in quiet tears, but my gritty hands were useless to wipe them away.

As I waited, I recalled the time when I had first seen Zeke among a crowd listening to Jesus. I had come with Lazarus. Being farther away from the Jordan shoreline, I could not hear Jesus, but it was enough to be with the throngs of people who were there to hear his teaching.

I remembered how Lazarus and I had walked from Mount Olive, then up to Jerusalem, and followed Jesus around for hours. We caught up with Jesus and many followers. Lepers at a distance were shouting plaintively, "Unclean." I felt sorry for them because they were outcasts even to their own families. Our neighbor Simon traveled afar and had said he was sometimes near lepers. I worried about him.

Beside the river, as the day wore on, I thought I would never get to see Jesus up close. We reached a cool grassy place beneath trees. As Jesus spoke, I could not hear him. People crowded next to him, and I could not see him. Lazarus did not try to push his way nearer. I saw other young women like myself among the throngs sitting beside their parents. It occurred to me many young women trailed after him and idolized him as I did, and I felt envious. I became more determined to buy the aromatic ointment I hoped Jesus would like. Baskets of fish and bread were being handed to people. Lazarus stood. "Mary, stay here. I want to go help distribute the food Jesus has blessed." He looked around and saw an older man who had a donkey laden with goods. "My name is Lazarus and this is my sister Mary. May I please trust you to see to my sister's safety."

"I am Zeke the Rug Man and I will see to her safety," he said with a smile. He patted his donkey.

I became fascinated with the number of different items the rug man had attached to his donkey's back. Mesh sacks revealed olive oil, wine, and vials of other liquids or spices. After the men spoke, Lazarus hurried toward the group of people near Jesus who were sitting down and eating.

Zeke nodded to me. "I can share the food I have. My brother went to help his friends distribute food and will bring some to me if there is any left. We brought one round of bread and some flasks of water. I would like to go with him, but I will wait," I said. Although men did not usually speak to women I thought it was permitted since he was given the responsibility of my care.

"Considering the throng of folks, I believe people are safer here in the back," he said.

I tried to see what was going on past the crowd. There were too many people. Even up on my toes, I couldn't see Jesus. I settled dejectedly onto the cool grass. Throngs of people rushed toward the front, and

I worried what Jesus would do if he was pressed to the brink of the water.

"I do not mean to be too bold or rude, but I see you have many things for sale there. Besides rugs, what have you?"

"Leather goods, jewels, scarves, some ointments and oils, wine."

"What kinds of ointments and oils?"

"Nice smelling things made from flowers and herbs. Most are very expensive, so don't tell anyone. I don't want to be robbed." He chuckled, then gradually lowered himself to a small brown rug he placed on the grass. He groaned a little. "I'm getting too old to sit on the earth most days. Are you interested in oils and ointments?"

"I want to buy something nice for a friend." I looked away, as I was almost certain I did not have enough money.

"I have a few kinds. Nard smells very nice, but is usually in a costly decorated clay vial. One breaks it open and applies it where needed to soothe. Women use it as perfume, but it is often used for anointing a body for burial."

"I wish I could smell it, but I would not want you to crack it open so I could get a whiff."

Zeke chuckled, then turned to me with a serious expression. "You seem like such a nice young girl. I hope your brother comes soon so you can get something to eat."

"Do you have food? I can share my portion of the

bread with you. It was freshly baked early yesterday before we left," I said.

"You are kind and generous, but I have some food," Zeke said. We sat quietly. There was a murmur of people talking and eating, and a steady thrum and swish of the river. The air smelled fresh and a little like fish. "You said you wanted to buy something special for a friend. He or she must be very important to you."

"Yes, he is. My brother Lazarus and sister Martha often invite him to our home. It is Jesus." The words were out, but I had not meant to tell anyone.

"You know the rabbi who is speaking to many people today? He is a remarkable teacher and even greater prophet. I like him." Zeke moved onto all fours and gradually got himself to an upright position and rolled his rug as if to leave.

"I'm glad you like him, too," I said. "He is wonderful, and I am disappointed I am so far back I can barely hear his words."

"I have a small plain jar of nard I may find difficult to sell to those who buy it to impress others. Since your friend is a man I admire, I can give you a good price."

I dug into my waist pouch and put the denarius in my palm so Zeke could see it. He went to the donkey and reached his hand into a bag that hung down one side. He lifted out the bulbous clay jar, which had no decoration save a tiny leaf carved into the clay. "It is more than enough." He smiled, as he gave it to me, took my coin, and gave me three leptons in change.

"Thank you." I was greatly pleased and I tucked the small, sealed nard container into the folds of my garment. I felt peaceful and content. It was as if YHWH had meant for me to meet Zeke the Rug Man and obtain the gift I would give to Jesus.

Back to reality, the storm had quieted and I heard Reuben exclaim, "Look below, my steed. The old man fell and got himself killed, as he has not moved. Perhaps the girl and his ass also perished down there amid the storm. Too bad, as I wanted to collect money from her uncle for finding her." Horse hooves clopped, galloping away, and I listened until the sound waned and disappeared.

I peered out. The air had become fresh and clear. Schnek huffed, and I breathed a sigh of thanksgiving when I saw Zeke clambering up to reach us, so we could retrieve his rugs and wares and be on our way again. My heart sang with relief.

"Do you think Reuben was sent by my Uncle Elias to find me?"

"No. I believe he was a man who had heard of your disappearance and was hoping to make money if he found you. I did not trust him."

"I agree. He was too rough on you and me. Uncle Elias would not have sent such a man to bring me home. I believe YHWH might have sent you looking for me." I helped Zeke shake the sand from the rugs.

His eyes twinkled with mirth. "I will make every effort

to bring you home to your family. As I have told you, I travel far and wide trading wares and especially rugs. One time I am here and another I find myself going off in a different direction. And yes, Mary, YHWH is my guide."

I pondered his words in my heart, trying to decide if he might be one of God's angels, but he did not fit into my picture of what an angel might look like. We had a long way to go to Jerusalem. Smiling, I kept my thoughts to myself. Reuben was still out there somewhere. I prayed we would not meet with the likes of Reuben again. Our faith would guide us.

20 Simon

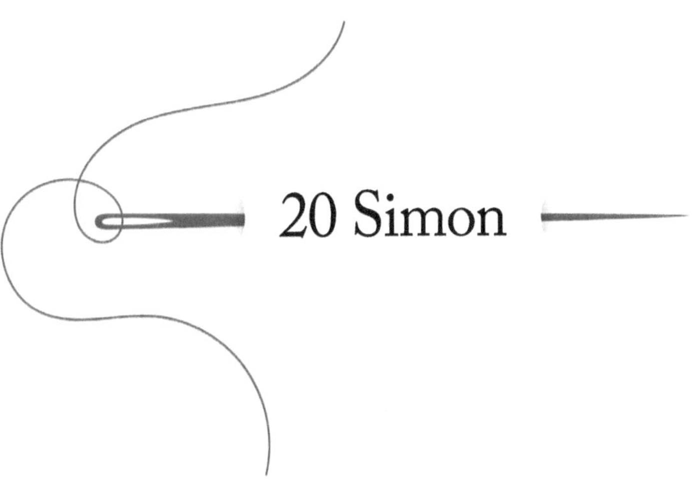

Happy are those whose strength is in you,
in whose heart are the highways to Zion.

Psalm 84:5

Lazarus and I hired a horse-drawn carriage from a man who owed me a favor. We could have made better time on two horses, but I wanted a way to bring Mary home as best we could. I only hoped we would find her well and not abused and broken. The man warned me, "Simon, the carriage may not travel well on some of the terrain, but you have the horse in any case."

Lazarus wanted to go toward Egypt over land, and we set out early one morning. The sky was clear blue with a few pillows of white clouds overhead. As the day wore on, we spoke of the Roman tyrants overseeing our people's every move. Taxes had been levied, which many could not pay, and they were sent to prison. If anyone, man, woman or child, was in the street when the Roman guard came marching through town, they scattered lest they be trampled or impaled. Despite these concerns, very little could dampen my spirits since I had been healed. I marveled at my clear hands.

After we had traveled a few days, we saw a man on a black horse coming toward us in the distance. I said, "I pray he is not someone hoping to rob us."

"May YHWH and Jesus protect us," Lazarus said.

The horseman came up to us and we stopped. "Greetings, I hope your travel is going well." His voice was deep, and he spoke with an accent, possibly Roman. He appeared tall and daunting atop the shiny black horse.

"We have hardly begun, this being the end of the second day," Lazarus said.

"Where are you going?"

"We are searching for my sister who has been missing for weeks. After receiving some clues, we think we are on our way to finding her," Lazarus said.

"Have you seen any young women on your way?" I asked.

"A few," he smiled knowingly. "I will keep a watch out for her." He had looked away while he spoke, then galloped off without another word. Dust floated in the air, and caused me to choke and cough.

"He was in some kind of hurry." Lazarus wiped his brow. We noticed the man rode off a way and then watched him double back.

"Yes," I said. "He did not introduce himself, did not speak fluent Aramaic, and I am inclined not to trust one such as him."

"His countenance looks like a Roman or possibly Philistine. At least he did not try to rob us." Lazarus looked at me earnestly.

We plodded along at a pace, then found a small pool where our horse could get water. A frog hopped out and startled us. No spring was nearby, and I did not trust the still mossy water to drink. We had flasks of wine and water so we were able to refresh ourselves.

The lay of the land changed as we rode. Some small bushes were along the trail, but it was mostly sand. The sun was hotter than I remembered, but I had been covered up for a long time while I had leprosy. And I decided to be joyful, rather than complain. My perspective had changed since the day I had first become leprous, faithless, and until the wonderful day I was healed by Jesus. Faith now stayed near, as I knew in my heart YHWH was with me, and I was forever grateful.

We came to a town with a sand brick wall, and an open gate where we replenished our supplies, talked with the townsfolk, and rested overnight. No one had seen Mary. We stayed with an old couple named Anna and Ephraim, who wanted us to stay longer. She supplied us with bread, cheese, and dried fruit for our journey and they bade us God's speed on our way. They were devout people.

When the town was far behind us we came to a difficult place on the trail, one where we did not think the carriage could make it without tipping over. "Lazarus, we should stop, and you take the carriage back to the town. I will continue on foot. When you have secured the carriage, ride the horse to catch up to me and we will go on searching."

"I fear leaving you alone, Simon," he said.

"All will be well with me. Go."

As he turned around and left me, I sent a prayer to YHWH to protect him and Mary, wherever she was, and last of all, me. Despite the sunshine, I felt a chill as I watched Lazarus disappear. I was alone in unfamiliar territory, a situation that had never troubled me when I was handling my business in foreign countries. Why did I feel vulnerable now? I trudged along and smelled the scent of animal dung. Would Lazarus find someone with whom to safely leave the carriage?

After a short while, I saw dust billowing in the distance, and hoped it was Lazarus returning. If it was the scoundrel we had encountered earlier, I was defenseless, save my faith YHWH was with me. After all, I was doing what I thought he wanted me to do, helping Lazarus search for Mary. Was this what Jesus meant when he told me to follow him?

Lazarus rode up. "Come on and ride with me. I think the horse can support both of us. After all, he was pulling a cart."

I tried hanging onto the horse's tail to hoist myself up, but faltered and fell to the ground. My arms and legs were weak from too many months of being ill and idle. It was no use. "I give up," I said, "go on without me."

"Simon, come on, you can do it." He alit from the horse. "Use the mane in front and hoist yourself up." He gave me his steady arms to help.

I felt older than my years as I obeyed my friend and finally got enough purchase to get my legs astraddle. I chuckled, apologetically. "Thank you."

We were on our way. Suddenly the horse reared up, and we both landed on the sand. I scraped an elbow and knee. Lazarus was sprawled on the ground. The horse was galloping away. We both got up as quickly as we could. I saw the cause of the horse's behavior. A snake was slithering away.

"How can we get our horse back?" I asked.

"I will try calling to him and walking slowly toward him as he has stopped running now."

We gradually regained the trust of the horse and rode on. After some days, we came to the border where we would cross the river into Egypt. Off in the distance, we saw what looked like a man, his donkey, and probably the man's wife. They were standing in silhouette. I felt pangs of jealousy, as I no longer had plans to marry as before my leprosy.

We kept to the trail and found a place in the river where it looked like the horse could go across. I wondered if he could handle both of us. "Let us cross one at a time, and send him back to get the other. You go first," I said.

Lazarus did not hesitate and they plunged into the Nile. I stepped back and watched. Lazarus got off of the horse and spoke to him. I called with a whistle and hand waving so he would see me even if he did not hear me. The horse stood on the bank, looking at the river for a long while. He huffed and would not budge into the river to come get me even though Lazarus tried to push him.

I looked where I had seen the couple and the donkey and they were still there but seemed to be moving slowly toward me. I wondered why they were traveling beside the river, not on the trail as we had been. Perhaps they had another direction in which they needed to travel. Were they going to go toward Jerusalem where we had come from?

Lazarus was still trying to coax the horse into the rolling stream. I wondered what we were going to do if the horse wouldn't budge. Could I swim across the stream? I thought not.

The couple with the donkey kept coming toward me. I hoped against hope they were good people. When they got closer I would ask them if they had come from Egypt, and if they had seen Mary. I divided my attention between the errant horse we were depending on for our travels and the approaching trio. Lazarus seemed to give up.

"YHWH, how soon will it be until we find Mary?" I lifted my voice and face toward the blue heavens.

Lazarus was mounting the horse. I watched as he kicked the horse's flanks. He was coming back across. I supposed Lazarus could see the people I saw. "How do ordinary people cross the river?" I asked aloud, though I was sure no one would hear me.

The couple were coming in my direction, and I hoped they would be friendly. I had very little money with me so was not a good candidate for robbery. I partially covered my head with my cowl as I had done when I had leprosy. What if I were to call out my old warning of unclean when they approached?

Lazarus had decided to come back across on the horse, but it was not going directly across. I thought of my predicament and decided it was worth a try to ask YHWH to intervene. Faith had brought me safe thus far and would make my path straight. Doubt would not be my best defense now. "Save us, YHWH," I whispered. My eyes were closed to whatever was going on around me.

I winked one eye open as I saw the couple and their donkey nearby. The small woman's face was covered out of modesty or against the bright sunlight. The man was old and wore a turban. I thought I had seen such a man on previous travels, but I had seen many people and could be mistaken.

Mounted on the horse, Lazarus remained in the rushing stream, trying to move across. I shut my eyes again until I heard the woman shriek.

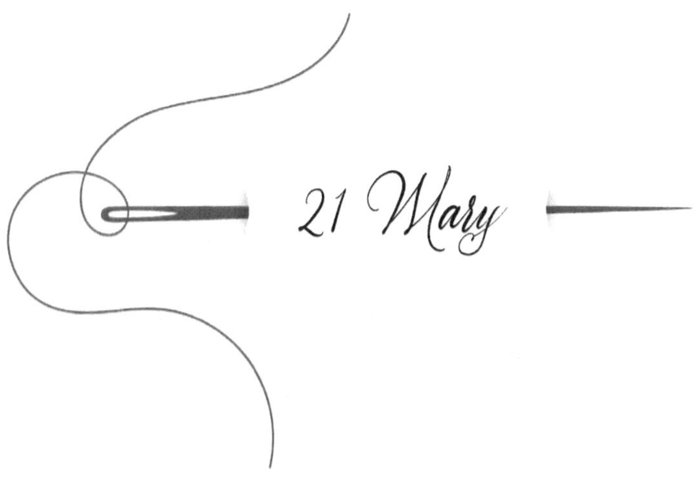

A friend loves at all times.

Proverbs 17:17a

Sunshine's shiny rays of the day had turned into the sun's final winking departure on the low-hilled rim of the earth. All I could think about was my homecoming. Every step I took brought me closer. No one was on the trail except an occasional farmer with an ox cart or laden donkey on their way to get supplies or bring them back. Each of these greeted us cordially and talked briefly about the weather "Nice day, a little cooler than yesterday."

My feet became weary, and my sandals had almost worn through the soles. I did not trouble Zeke with the complaint, but he noticed what had happened to my left sandal strap. Shortened and worn from wear, my sandal flapped untied as I walked, threatening to trip me. He stopped Schnek, and said, "Mary, I have a little gift for you."

I looked up as he untied a sack dangling from his donkey's back. He brought out a pair of sandals. "Will these fit you?"

"Oh, thank you, Zeke!" Tears of joy filled my eyes. YHWH surely had blessed me to have someone like a father accompanying me home. "My sister and I will prepare such a feast for you when we get home. And we will give you whatever you ask or need."

"My dear little Mary, I do not need anything from you. It is my pleasure to give you a pair of sandals so you do not have to walk barefoot on the hot sand. I am sorry I did not see your plight sooner. Why did you not say something?"

"I had no money and I did not want to trouble you."

"You are a considerate young woman, and I have been enjoying your companionship as we go."

"Do you know how far we are from Jerusalem?"

"Many more days. Once we have crossed the river out of Egypt we will be around fourteen sunsets walking until we arrive at your home."

"Thank you." There were no trees nearby, only brush and drying green grass, but I saw a rustle in the grass and heard little chirping noises. I was sure it must be a nest of chicks and I smiled.

"Do you need to rest?" Zeke had started walking again.

"No, I am enjoying the feel of new sandals on my feet, and the more steps I take, the sooner I will be home."

A town appeared in the distance near the end of the day. It seemed small at first, but as we came close I could see it was walled, with a gate and sentry. "Where are we?"

"It could be Memphis, a good place to stop for the night."

When we came to the gate, Zeke spoke to the guard in a language I did not know. He later told me it was Greek. We stayed in the home of a couple Zeke knew named Mameta and Nicholas. Schnek stayed in their stable. I was given a blanket in the corner of the room by the hearth, and Zeke was housed on the roof to sleep.

I awakened to the mouthwatering aroma of food being prepared, the sound of a kettle being moved from where it dangled over the coals of the hearth. When she saw me sit up, Mameta gave me a cheery, "Oh-ho."

"God's good morning," I said. I knew she probably got

the message from the happy sound of my voice. I smelled fish cooking with vegetables and herbs. A young woman came in the back door carrying loaves of freshly baked bread. The aroma was so much like home, like manna from heaven YHWH had provided to our ancestors. I almost shed tears. I could hardly wait to get to Bethany.

After we ate and were on our way, Zeke said the Nile would be difficult to walk across, even in the low place where we were going. "What will we do?" I looked up at him, hoping he had a way to get us safely across.

"A man who has a flat wood boat may put Shnek on it with us and we can get across if he is working when we get there. It is a little dangerous, I hear."

"I do not know how to swim," I said.

'Oh, we will get across with little worry of tipping into the current of the river," he said.

Nonetheless, I fretted. When we got to the bank of the river, a friendly man named Daniel was there with the flat boat. His cloak was simple, and he wore natural-color trousers like those worn by fishermen. He had a rope to tie Shnek, so he wouldn't fall off the boat. The man talked at length to Zeke, who took everything off Shnek's back. He put it into baskets and tied them to the raft. The load was light as rugs had been sold in Memphis. When we tried to get Shnek onto the flat surface of the boat, which was already in the water, he balked. He brayed loudly and huffed at Daniel and Zeke. I did not know what we were going to do. Shnek forcefully broke loose and plunged into the river.

"Oh, no," I gasped in horror. Shnek took some time to get his bearings but miraculously made his way across the river to wait for us on the other side. He shook himself as if glad to have gotten a bath. I laughed but realized we needed to be taken across. The man grabbed oars and bade us get onto his small fishing boat, and all the baskets of items were on as well. He rowed but did not get us directly across as the current drove us downstream. I was fearful, remembering my time on the open sea when I was being taken to Egypt and sold into slavery. My stomach was upset and my chest resounded with loud thumps as if I ran.

Somehow, we managed to get to the riverbank on the other side. Schnek trotted over to us as Zeke reached into his waist pouch and paid Daniel what he had asked without haggling about the price. He reached inside a sack of grain and fed Shnek.

Silently, I prayed to YHWH to direct us. What would happen if I lost faith now? "Where are we?" I asked after Zeke settled and secured his wares on Shnek's back.

Zeke looked around in all directions. "We are no longer in Egypt. I have been here before . . ." He paused, distracted, and I could see why. In the distance, a man was standing on the shore waving to a man with a horse on the opposite side. It was a dark horse like the one Rueben had been riding.

What I saw made my eyes fill with tears. I could hardly believe my eyes as I saw my brother atop a horse in the Nile River. Only then did I notice the man who waited for him on the bank. He looked like our neighbor Simon. He could be a leper, as he was covered with a cloak from head to foot. I wondered at his accompanying my brother. My life pulse beat hard as if to burst out of my body. I screamed, "Lazarus! Lazarus, is it you, or am I dreaming?"

22 Simon

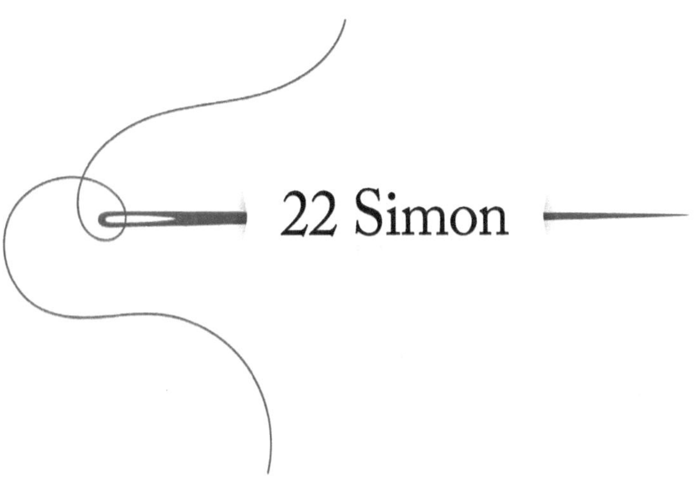

Sing aloud to God our strength;
shout for joy to the God of Jacob.

Psalm 81:1

Lazarus whooped out, "Mary, Mary, I am here!" His words were swallowed by the wind as he pushed forward. With mighty leaps, the horse plunged on across. Lazarus rode the horse and alit dripping. "Mary, you are alive and safe now with me," he said. His damp arms were around Mary as if she was the most precious thing in the world and he could lose her any second. He had kissed her cheeks and the top of her head. They were together, brother and sister, and it was enough.

Zeke looked on with a bemused smile. "Greetings, I am Zeke, the Rug Man, and very happy to see you two reunited."

"Lazarus from Bethany." He clasped shoulders with Zeke. "Thank you for whatever hand you have had in bringing her here safely."

I was almost speechless. I came close, cowl dropped to my shoulders to reveal a clear-skinned face. I greeted Zeke. "My name is Simon. Lazarus and I are neighbors. I used to have leprosy, but I was healed by Jesus. After my healing, I dedicated my time to helping others in any way I could, and I insisted on coming with him to search for his sister."

"I met Mary after she had escaped from the man who had bought her from the slavers. She is a clever one and a good travel companion." Zeke held onto his donkey's rein, smiling.

"Her sister Martha will be very excited to see her. We must all have a feast when we get back to Bethany. Zeke, are you going to Jerusalem?" Lazarus said.

"Yes, I will go along with all of you and trade wares as I can. I travel many places and have only general plans. When I need to go on, I do." Zeke's blue eyes glowed with a faraway gaze.

"Simon, I heard you tell Zeke you were cured of leprosy by Jesus. Praise him. He is the one who calls himself the Son of Man. I never stopped believing I would be rescued. I will soon give you all the terrible details of my capture, being sold, and how I miraculously escaped," Mary said, breathless from excitement.

Lazarus cupped his hands, motioning for Mary to come, step up, and get on the horse. "Let us be on our way now. We can pick up the carriage we left and then hurry on our way to Bethany."

"I will try to keep up." Zeke's eyes twinkled.

Mary said, "Simon, I am so grateful to you for coming with my brother. YHWH has blessed you with healing. Even if we do not arrive in Bethany at the same time, we will make a feast and invite all the followers of Jesus and our neighbors."

"Martha is a wonderful cook, and I look forward to it." We traveled together at a walking pace, with Lazarus leading the horse Mary rode, and Zeke leading his donkey. I thought nothing in the world could dampen our joy.

When we arrived at the town where the carriage had been left, Lazarus and I went to the man who had promised to keep it until he got back.

"I do not have your carriage. A man riding a black

horse came and said he was getting the carriage for you. He paid for a half-day's storage but said you would pay for the remainder of it when you arrived."

"He was lying," I said. "I wonder how he knew we left a carriage here."

"We are a small town, so it was not difficult for him to find out if a carriage was stowed here."

"It must have been the scoundrel who tried to take Mary from my care," said Zeke.

"He was on a black steed."

"I did not trust the man. We saw him, too, on our way, and I saw him turn back," I said.

"He hardly spoke with us and had the accent of a Philistine. He evaded our question of whether he had seen Mary." Lazarus scowled.

Lazarus and I haggled with the man who had stored the carriage until he took only a part of the money he asked for initially. Now, there was no carriage to ride in back home, not to mention our debt to the man who had provided it to us in Jerusalem.

We replenished provisions, watered the horse and donkey, and went on our way, too upset to spend time in the town after what had happened.

It was a long journey, lasting more than fourteen sunsets. Still, time went quickly for me as Mary entertained us with the details of her capture, ride across the sea with another captive, Carabel, the slavers selling the two young girls to Master Arthrimian, her escape, and recent happenings.

We became more and more excited the closer we got to Jerusalem, and when I saw the familiar rise of the temple mount in the distance I knew we were home, I prayed a prayer of deep thanksgiving to YHWH, and Jesus. The sun shone brightly, but even if it had been raining, nothing could quench my spirits.

23 Mary

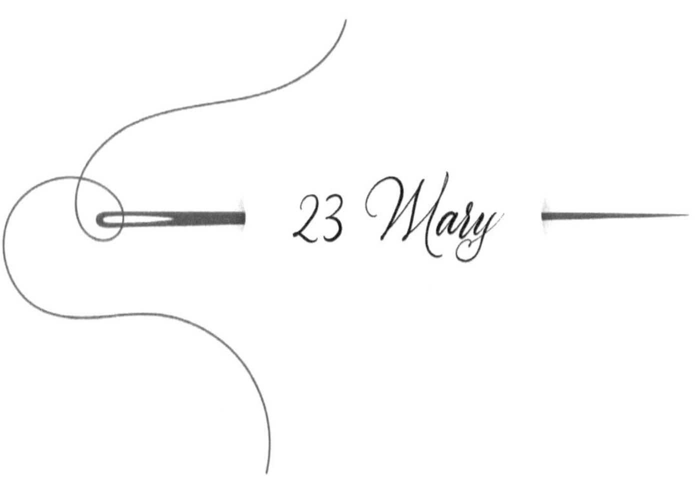

Answer me, O Lord, for your steadfast love is good;
according to your abundant mercy, turn to me.
Do not hide your face from your servant, for I
am in distress – make haste to answer me.

Psalm 69:16–17

We came near a man herding a flock of sheep. He waved and looked up at me on the horse, then looked away. I wondered if it was Carabel's father as she had told me they were shepherds. "I regret leaving her," I said quietly to myself.

Martha had received word from Ott of our impending return. He had heard of our coming by people we met on the way who had seen us. As our small procession entered Jerusalem and went on the Mount Olive Trail, neighbors asked about our travels. Some had known of my disappearance and were glad to see me reunited with my brother. By the time we were in Bethany, my sister had already prepared a special meal for us.

Arms open, Martha met us halfway down the trail. We embraced and clung to each other as never before. The shoulder of my tunic became damp as we wept together out of sheer happiness and thankfulness. Simon went to his house to see Ott and his family and freshen up. Lazarus came in a little later as he had settled with the man from whom he had originally hired the horse and carriage.

At Martha's insistence, all of us had a wonderful lamb stew, vegetables, cheese, bread, and dried and fresh fruits. We had honey date cakes and wine. Our joy at being together continued as we talked. We raised our cups of wine, "To life! Shalom!"

Lazarus lay down on his bed in the corner of the great room. In only a few moments, he was asleep. I tried to get him to come back to the table and eat date cakes with us, but he was sound asleep. We all understood. Zeke and Simon were both tired, and Simon asked Zeke to come stay in his house. The donkey, Schnek, was tied in the courtyard. Zeke came to tell us he was leaving the next morning. As I bid him a safe journey, I stood on tiptoe to kiss his cheeks and thank him. I had the nicest sensation, as if I had touched an angel. I had never kissed a sacred being or thing, but it was how I felt about dear old Zeke.

Martha wanted to hear everything and kept asking me if I wanted more food. After giving her some of the details of my experiences, I left her and sank into my lamb's wool bed. She said, "It is a miracle you are home, and a miracle Simon was healed to go search for you. Tomorrow we will have more time to talk when you are refreshed."

The next morning, it was clear to us something was amiss with Lazarus. He sipped a little broth, but would not eat. "It is alright. I am only very tired from the trip." He looked pale, and his brow remained furrowed.

I sat with him. "Thank you so much for finding me. I never lost faith you or Jesus would come for me. Rest and be well."

"Thank Simon too. He is a very good man." Lazarus's voice was hoarse.

Lazarus did not recover. He became more ill. "Where is Jesus?" I wondered.

"Walking somewhere, sharing his message of love, healing people," he answered weakly.

"He needs to come heal you," Martha said.

Simon came to see how we were. "How is it you are ill after such a wonderful reunion with little Mary?"

"Do not worry. I will be well." Lazarus's voice was a whisper.

"Simon, please send word to Jesus. Lazarus is very ill. He must come and heal him," Martha's voice was deep with urgency, and her brow was furrowed with concern.

"I will," Simon said. He left to send a runner to find Jesus.

I kept my vigilance, trying to get Lazarus to eat something, drink a little broth or wine, but he would have only small sips until one day he stopped. "Lazarus, please try to take a little nourishment. Jesus is on his way, and when he gets here, you will be healed." It had been a few days since Simon had sent the runner. I wondered at the delay.

The next morning, I awakened to Martha's uncontrollable weeping. Lazarus had died.

I wept and tore my sleeve, unbearably wretched. Besides mourning my brother, I was sad and deeply disappointed Jesus had let us down. He had healed others, why could he not be troubled to heal one of his best friends? With help from neighbors, Uncle Elias, Martha, and I did what we needed to bury his body. Cleansing, anointing, and wrapping with cloth. Simon and neighbor men laid him in our family's tomb and closed it with a large stone. We were all ritually unclean after having touched his body. After we cleansed in our mikveh, we sat shiva.

I despaired and ripped the other sleeve of my tunic. It would be another to mend if I cared to do it. Simon tried to console me, but I shook my head. I was sick at heart wondering why Jesus had abandoned us when we needed him the most. Perhaps I had been wrong about Jesus all along. Four days passed after my brother died. I was miserable and angrier than ever.

Neighbors were sitting with Martha, Uncle Elias, and me as was the custom for seven days following a death. Food was brought in by Ott's wife Naomi and other friends, but I did not feel like eating anything. How could this have happened?

Martha went out of the house and down the trail, and I heard her voice echoing excitedly. Next, I heard others murmuring. Martha came back to me. "Jesus is coming. Come meet him."

"Why meet him now Lazarus is dead? I do not want to speak with him." Teary-eyed, reluctantly, I got up. I was not sure what to say to Jesus. It was too late for him to do anything. People who loved Lazarus were all weeping. Uncle Elias had torn his tunic in despair and wore a black band on his sleeve. Suddenly, Jesus was beside me. "Why do you weep?"

"If you had been here, my brother would not have died." I did not look at him as I sniffed into a cloth wet with tears.

Jesus touched my shoulder, and then he began to weep.

"See how he loved him," Simon uttered.

"Show me where you have laid him," Jesus said. We walked down to the tomb. A large stone secured it. He commanded, "Remove the stone."

"Why bother? He has been dead four days, and there will be a stench." Annoyed and sorely grieved, Martha already had a scented cloth applied to her nose.

"Roll the stone away." Jesus's voice repeated his command. Ott and two disciples obeyed him.

By now, many curious onlookers had come, including Pharisees, Sadducees, and other officials. The stone was removed, and Jesus cried out in a loud voice, "Lazarus, come out!"

I shook with dread, wondering what Jesus was up to. We were all startled beyond belief when my brother slowly emerged almost unable to walk, wrapped in grave cloths. Jesus said, "Free him from the shroud cloths. Give him something to eat."

I was awestricken and forgave Jesus for delaying in coming to heal Lazarus. It was a miracle we had not anticipated. My brother who had been dead was alive. He was walking and using his hands to help Ott and John unwrap the grave bindings. Naomi hurried home and brought a robe to put on him. The onlookers were amazed, murmuring praises. "How did Jesus do it? Is he the Messiah, the son of YHWH?" someone asked.

Other murmurings could be heard. Then a Pharisee

said, "We have seen him flaunt laws before. It must have been another deception of his. Surely the man was not dead but asleep from strong drink. We must tell the authorities."

Six days before Passover, Jesus came to our house to sup. Martha and I put on an elaborate meal of fish, fresh bread, cheese, dates, lentil stew with chunks of lamb, bitter and sweet herbs, and red wine. Followers, including neighbor Simon, joined us for this meal. Jesus sat next to Lazarus and John.

I heard Lazarus thanking Jesus. He said, "Thank you, Jesus. I do not know how or why my life was restored, but I am a new man. I cannot explain it. It is as if I was only half alive before my death and return to life. I am noticing all the little blessings as I awake each day. Breezes play with leaves and sunlight illuminates and captivates light and dark colors all around us. Birds sing. I watch my sisters at work and marvel at their sweet faces intent on cooking or mending. I appreciate my family more than ever. I do not know what our Lord wants me to do with the rest of my life, but I trust I will discover it in time."

I marveled at what I heard my brother profess. I, too, sensed I had a new life since I safely left my captor, restored to my family and friends. It was as if I also had been dead and raised. I had a renewed appreciation of life. Simon's servants helped Martha and kept putting another dish on the table and plates for the extra guests. The kettle on our hearth was of a large capacity and the stew was almost to the brim. Ott's wife had a similar kettle going on Simon's hearth. Delicious smelling food aromas filled the air. I helped Martha, but soon I could contain myself no longer. I had been waiting for a time to give Jesus the nard I had long ago purchased from Zeke the Rug Man. I wanted to do something special for him. More people were seated in our common courtyard by Simon's place and were served there. Once when I looked up, I caught Simon looking intently at me and I averted my gaze.

Everyone was deep in conversation as I slipped away for a moment to bring out the anointing perfume. My hands shook with excitement before I broke the seal of the nard container on the stone floor. I stood beside Jesus and anointed his head first. He looked up at me surprised and amused, as drops of it shone on his eyebrows and trickled down his nose. The sunlight stream created a hallowed glow around his head. Then I knelt at his feet and poured the remainder of it there. The buzz of conversation stopped. All eyes were on Jesus and me. I shed happy tears on his feet. I had not brought a towel but loosened my long, dark hair to wipe the excess. Nard's exquisite scent wafted in the air.

An agitated disciple asked, "What is she doing?"

"Lord, you ought to chastise the woman for wasting a costly perfume. We could have sold it and given the money to the poor," said Judas of Iscariot. He shook a finger at me, pointing out what he judged to be a serious error on my part.

"The poor will always be with you, but not me. Leave Mary alone. None of you bathed my feet when I came here. Yet she has washed them with perfume and tears."

"Foolishness of women," scoffed someone.

"She has anointed me for my burial," Jesus said as he smiled and shook his gleaming head good-naturedly.

I must have looked awful with tears streaming down my cheeks, tangled flowing hair, and red eyes. I stopped wiping his feet and looked up at him. An aura surrounded him, and his long beautiful hair shone. I did not understand what he was talking about. I trust nobody knew except him what was to take place.

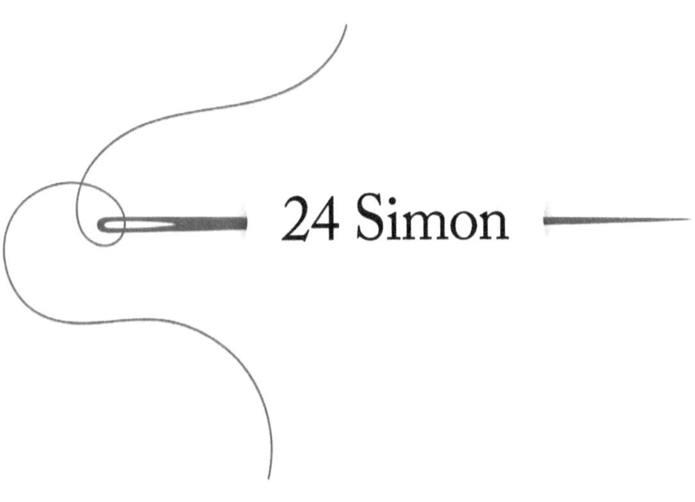

24 Simon

I will give thanks to the Lord with my whole heart;
I will tell of all your wonderful deeds

Psalm 9:1

While it was no longer the most important aspect of my life, it had been rewarding to get back to my business. The rock-cut tomb in the vale at the base of Mount Olive my workers had finished for the family who had contracted me to do it. It was crafted artistically and well done. The entryway of Greek style columns and round closure stone completed it. More tomb-cutting business came my way as a result. I quickly contracted the crew to carve more family tombs. I felt whole again. Whole, except for the emptiness at having given up my intended bride while I had leprosy. She was recently promised to a fortunate man. I wanted to select another woman. I thought of little Mary, but Martha being her elder ought to be considered first.

At supper with Martha, Lazarus, Jesus, and many followers, there was much discussion about my having been healed of leprosy, a miracle. Of course, the more outstanding miraculous feat had been the raising of Lazarus from the dead. We both were new men, with more life to live.

Mary had been so overcome with joy, she had anointed Jesus before we began to eat. I looked at her sweet face, aglow with loving adoration, and wished in my heart she would find me even half as attractive. She loved and adored Jesus. He had said something which brought a cloud of mystery amid the heady aroma of nard. I heard him say, "She has anointed me for burial." Was it a portent of things to come? He had not endeared himself to the Temple authorities, and the Romans, threatened by his popularity, wanted him stopped as well.

I heard whisperings among scribes and Pharisees afterwards. "The girl was sold into slavery and was a man's concubine. She should not even be near the Rabbi Jesus, much less touching him. What kind of life will she now have?"

Mary had assured me and Lazarus she had not been in the arms of the man who bought her but had escaped before anything bad happened. No other man had touched her. As I thought about Mary, she no longer seemed like "little Mary." All she had been through had matured her, so she was now a gracious young woman. If Martha had not prepared her sister for life, her recent challenges had. I wondered how to approach her Uncle Elias and Lazarus. I hoped someone had not already spoken for little Mary. I sensed Jesus was not a mere man ready for marriage, but someone entirely more extraordinary. Martha had denied all suitors after her espoused had died before the wedding ceremony. I wondered if she was still intent on remaining single and continuing to serve others with her diaconate work.

What would please Elias? We had been neighbors for years and I had known Mary since her childhood. My mind was full of ideas on how to speak with her uncle, but none of them stayed to fruition. Perhaps it was an idle proposal I could not stop thinking about.

The next morning as I sat on the stone bench in our courtyard prepared for prayer, I draped my prayer shawl over my whole body so I was not distracted by my surroundings. I thanked YHWH for my life and asked Him to direct me in the way I should now approach Elias to ask for Mary or Martha. I did not know if I should deign to ask the creator of all things, but I thought it was worth a try. I believed He had used Jesus to cure me and to bring Lazarus back to life.

It was as if YHWH smiled on the earth at this moment. As I sat praying ritual words in our mutual courtyard, the sun cast its warmth over me, and I felt comforted like being swaddled in a blanket. My leprous days were now a sad memory. I finished prayers and took the draped prayer cloth off my head to gaze about. I felt a gentle breeze, heard the little chirps of birds in the trees, and the door to the neighbor's house swung open. Mary stood and lifted her hands above her head, humming. I sat still, taking in all the beauty of the morning, especially her, and hoped it was an omen of good things to come.

I went to Elias's door and knocked.

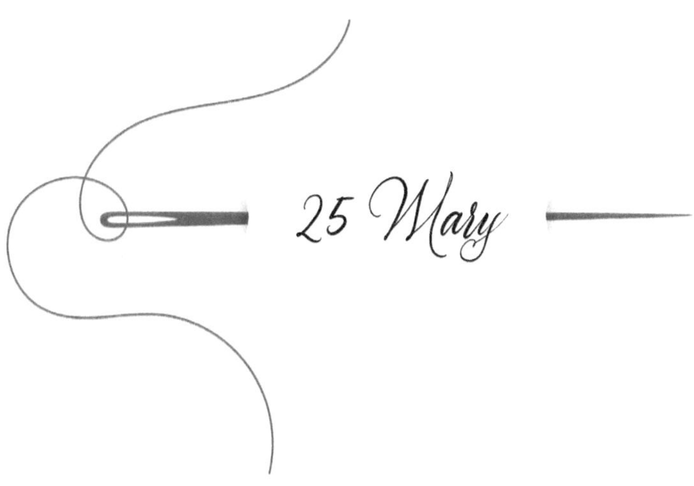

25 Mary

And he will destroy on this mountain the shroud that is cast over all peoples, the sheet that is spread over all the nations; he will swallow up death forever. Then the Lord God will wipe away tears from all faces, and the disgrace of his people he will take away from all the earth, for the Lord has spoken.

Isaiah 25:7–8

As I awakened another day in my home, it felt as if I had been given a new life and thanked YHWH. I was safe with my sister, brother, Uncle Elias nearby, and neighbors like Simon I had known since childhood. Jesus had raised my brother from the dead, and I adored him. Today, I would ask Uncle Elias if he would inquire of Jesus's parents for me to marry Jesus. I knew I should not be so bold, but I wanted to know what the future held. I imagined Jesus taking over his father's carpentry business, or starting his own trade in Sepphoris. His family was probably ready to see him settle down and stop going around stirring up trouble with the authorities.

Simon was such a caring man to have come searching for me. I watched him in our common court remove his fringed shawl after finishing his private prayers, and was very grateful Jesus had made him well. Simon was home in Bethany at the moment, but he had business travel and demands of his trade deals to attend. I smelled the bread baking in our oven. With me having been afar, I appreciated all the simple things in life I had always taken for granted before my abduction by the slavers. I shuddered, thinking of the awful cart and the peril I had escaped.

Simon left his bench in the courtyard he used as his place of prayer, nodded to me, and smiled. "Shalom."

"Shalom, Simon."

I went to the side of the house and used the special shovel to take the bread from our oven. I folded the loaves into the skirt of my garment to bring them inside. The bread looked and smelled wonderful. I never wanted to leave home again for any reason. When next year our spring dried up, Lazarus would have to go down for water. I shuddered, thinking of what I had been through. The ordeal had helped me to grow in my appreciation towards my family and friends and gave me a sense of self. I was no longer the silly idle Mary who thought mostly of herself.

"Martha, here is bread," I said, as I skipped into our house.

"Thank you, Mary. We will break our fast in a moment when the eggs are done. Lazarus has already gone into Jerusalem to meet with Jesus and his followers, so it is only us unless Uncle Elias will join us."

"I will see." I hurried out. I heard voices and realized Simon was there. I hesitated, then knocked. The conversation stopped inside.

"Mary," Uncle Elias said. "What brings you here this early?"

"We have fresh bread and eggs if you would like some."

"Simon is here, and we were discussing some business." He had a twinkling smile in his brown eyes. "I will be there as soon as we are through."

"Oh, thank you. Please ask Simon if he wants to sup with us."

In a short while, Simon and Uncle Elias sat at the table with us, and we talked about the beautiful day we were enjoying. Simon was quiet, so I presumed he was thinking of trade and business. A short while after eating, they left.

After I cleared the table and washed dishes, I sat outside in a patch of sunlight and mended our torn tunic sleeves. I thought it was a perfect day. Nothing could dampen my joy. Martha hummed as she cleaned the house. Gentle breezes greeted me in our courtyard, birds twittered overhead, and some tiny yellow flowers bloomed brightly among the greenery. The scent of a new-mown field drifted from somewhere and filled the air. "Mending again," I said.

Martha cane outside. "It is the way of life," she said. "We are born, we die, we tear our tunics in grief, and then we mend and go on with life."

I pondered her words, taking careful stitches as I restored an almost torn off sleeve.

Lazarus returned late in the day. His brow furrowed, and he kept shaking his head as if something troubled him.

"What is wrong?" I asked.

"I cannot talk any sense into Jesus. He is right, of course in his assessment of those in power, their misinterpretation of the Torah, and the unjust Temple money-changing practices. But if they arrest him, bind him in chains, or worse, he will not be able to continue his teachings."

"It would be so awful for him and his family. Is there anything I can do?"

"No, Mary. He will have to do whatever he needs to do by himself. He and his disciples are going away to pray. He calls YHWH his father. When you pray, pray Jesus will be protected."

I looked with kindness at my brother, and decided he was not thinking clearly. We had been sorely tested recently ourselves. "Jesus will be alright." I patted my brother's shoulder, feeling helpless. Gloom prevailed in our household, and little more was said.

After I washed dishes with Martha, put kitchen items in order, I sat in a patch of sunlight and continued to do some mending. I tried not to worry about Jesus. Lazarus went to talk with Uncle Elias concerning the political unrest in Jerusalem.

When I stepped into the common courtyard to take a breath, a man was seated next to Simon on the stone bench. They both stood. "Greetings, Mary, I would like you to meet another cured leper, Lemuel. He was my friend among the tombs when we were both suffering the disease. He has told me he is back with his wife and children. He had left them in the care of his brother when he got leprosy as he thought he would never be well and fit to be a husband and father to them again. We praise Jesus and YHWH for our healing."

"It is wonderful you are both well and restored. Simon, you were betrothed to someone." I left my questions unspoken.

He cleared his throat and shook his head. "I had to break the promise with her parents as I did not know I would ever be well. She is espoused to another. But I am grateful to see Lemuel once more. We have been discussing ways he and I might work on business endeavors together. He has gone back to his home and family and his work of repairing houses and household tables and chairs made of wood or metal."

"Happy for you both." I decided to go back inside and leave the two friends alone.

Lazarus came in, grabbed some bread and cheese to eat, and slung his cloak over one shoulder. "I'm off to Jerusalem again, so do not wait sup for me."

"Shall I come too?" I was perplexed about the things he had said were happening there concerning Jesus and the authorities, and wished I could be there to comfort Jesus with my presence.

"No, Mary, you must not come. It is too perilous. Please do not follow me, as it could get very bad there." His eyes flashed.

"I will listen to your warning and stay home. If it is so threatening perhaps you should not go." I hung my head but heeded the counsel of my brother. I wanted no more trouble for myself. I stood at the front door and watched him go down the trail until it curved and took him out of my sight. I pulled my scarf to cover most of my head and breathed a silent prayer of protection for Lazarus, Jesus, Jesus's followers, and his family.

So much had recently happened in my life. I thought about the naïve "little flower" I had been the day I was abducted. Since then, I had learned to live by my wits and had deepened my faith in YHWH. While I did not know what the future held, I knew I would not live in my sister's house forever.

Had a whole day passed? Outside, men's voices rumbled. Upset, angry, or in anguish, I could not tell which. Our courtyard was normally a quiet haven for visits where gentle breezes and birds were heard among olive branches. I feared what trouble was causing so much discord.

Lazarus came into the house and admonished Martha and me to stay inside as there was trouble going on in the area, especially Jerusalem. "Does it concern Jesus, and is he going to do something about it?"

"It is all about Jesus and the authorities, both Temple and Roman. Please hear me. You must both remain inside the house here in Bethany. Some of his followers and I are going back to see whether we can do anything to stop what is happening."

"Please, what is happening?"

"They have arrested him, but I believe if Jesus wishes, he can stay away from them even so. He was powerful enough to restore my life." Lazarus kissed the top of my head and left.

Time passed, but Lazarus did not return. Simon was gone, probably on business, but I did not know. I prayed nothing bad would befall Jesus or his mother, my brother, the followers, and my neighbor Simon.

Uncle Elias came to sup with us but had little to say. I caught him looking at me as if deep in thought, perhaps remembering how he used to put this little niece on his shoulders and walk down to the town, chanting songs all the way. I saw a bemused smile on his lips as he ate his soup. We celebrated Passover in an unusual way, only at home, without Lazarus. It had been so strange not to go into Jerusalem to the Temple courtyard, or to the synagogue. While I was thankful to be with my family and not in a foreign place, bitter herbs this year meant more than I knew. When Lazarus came home after being away longer than we had expected, his shoulders slumped, his garment sleeve ripped as one who mourns. I knew something terrible had happened to a dear friend, and I hoped it was not Jesus. He flung himself onto his mat and gave in to deep wrenching sobs and groaning.

I was afraid to ask what had happened.

Late in the evening, Uncle Elias came, appearing distressed as if the worst had occurred. Someone had told him, so he came to be with us. He swallowed hard, and said, "Jesus has been crucified, and they laid him in a tomb."

Today was Sabbath. He had been crucified yesterday. I tore my tunic sleeve I had mended recently, and I wept bitterly, wondering how it could have happened. He had cured lepers and raised Lazarus. Why had YHWH forsaken him? None of us could understand. "Where are his disciples? Did they not put up a fight?"

Lazarus said, "Soldiers were there and threatening. His mother and followers are all in hiding, fearful we could experience the same fate."

A while later, Simon came into our house. He sat quietly near Uncle Elias. Martha put food on the table for everyone. She kept her hands busy, especially when she was distressed. I should have helped her but saw nothing else needed to be done.

"Where have they laid him?" Martha asked.

"In a tomb given for his use by Joseph, a Pharisee from Arimathea. Joseph's family lived here for a time, and he does business in many places," Simon said. "Joseph believed in Jesus's teachings. My stonecutters created his family tomb years ago."

"I want to go and anoint his body," I said.

"You cannot remove such a huge stone to add spices to his body," Martha said. "It is not safe for you to go out."

Simon, sleeve torn in mourning, came near to me. "Mary, we all loved him. I know how you must be grieving the same as all of us."

I could not answer him as I was too distraught. I sobbed uncontrollably, certain he had no understanding of how I felt. The table piled with fish, dried fruits, cheese, and bread remained untouched.

Nothing would ever be the same again. "Lazarus, please let me go tomorrow to see where they laid the body of Jesus. Come with me, as I need to go see the place. Is his mother in Jerusalem? Is anyone sitting shiva with her?"

"I am certain her friends and family are sitting with her."

The next morning before sunrise, I walked down the trail alone, not knowing how I would find the tomb. I was not fearful. Mary the mother of Jesus and her companions were hurrying along, and I asked if I could come with them. Each of us had some ointment or spice we had intended to put on his body. We did not know how we would get inside the tomb as gravestones, though often round, were large and heavy.

I hurried ahead and was joined by Mary of Magdala. The earth shook beneath our feet, but we kept running. When we got to the tomb we were astonished to see the stone was rolled to one side. Roman guards lay asleep outside.

We were frightened but tiptoed into the tomb. The grave cloths were folded neatly on the stone bench, but his body was not there. We both stood in awe and quietly shook our heads as the other women joined us.

"Someone stole his body!" Mary of Magdala remarked. Others echoed the same sentiments. "Where have you laid him?" she asked the large sentinel dressed in white who stood there.

"The one you look for is not here." Even though in the dark cave, the sentinel glowed as if in bright sunlight as he spoke. When I looked away for a moment he had left.

Except for Mary of Magdala, my companions hurried off saying, "Unless his body was stolen, perhaps he has risen like he said he would. We must go tell the others."

Mary of Magdala and I sat in the dew-kissed garden and wept, wanting to believe the sentinel, but afraid to. A man, whom I thought was the gardener, walked among the lush green bushes and flowering plants. He asked, "Why do you weep?"

"They have stolen the body of my Lord," Mary said.

"Do not weep for me, Mary and Mary."

I gasped, almost unable to believe my ears. "My teacher, my Lord, Jesus it is you." I could not touch him. Mary of Magdala and I knelt at his feet to kiss them, but he was gone as suddenly as he had appeared. Mary and I ran to find the others and tell them the wonderful news. "I have seen him. He is alive!"

The fearful disciples were hidden away. Some men we saw on the streets scoffed at our announcement. "Women can be so excitable. They probably looked inside the wrong tomb."

"His followers stole the body to make everyone think he rose from the dead," said a man who wore the rich robe of a Pharisee. I wanted to disprove what the scoffers said but decided they were not going to listen to a woman.

I never saw Jesus again. He appeared to his followers who were in a locked room and showed them his healed wounds so they would know it was him and nobody else. I heard tell Jesus also appeared to five hundred people. His apostles were filled with the Holy Spirit and he admonished them to go and tell people about his life, death, and resurrection from the dead. I was deeply saddened. While I mended our torn garments, I tried to remember the good as well as conduct my life as Jesus would have wanted. Life goes on in the midst of tearing and mending in spite of circumstances.

Jesus taught us about love. He loved us and laid down his life for us so we might all live well here on earth and on into eternity with him. I believed it instantly and wanted to go and proclaim the good news to everyone, but I did not know how I would do it.

Several weeks passed. Then one day, we prepared what seemed like an ordinary meal except my Uncle Elias had provided a stone jar of a special red wine, and was more jovial than usual. He and Simon sat at our table on the stone benches with Lazarus, Martha, and me. Our wine goblets had been refilled by Martha. "Simon has a request, and I will allow him to speak first," said Uncle Elias.

Martha and I hushed our chatter and Simon said, "I am here to ask Uncle Elias to promise Mary to me as my wife. I asked first for Martha, but your Uncle Elias has declined on her behalf, as she is devoted to her diaconate work and does not desire marriage."

I was stunned into complete silence. I liked Simon and thought well of him, but I had been in love with Jesus who turned out to be the son of YHWH and not anyone who would marry. I wanted to serve YHWH the rest of my life and had not thought about marriage. Perhaps my face, though flushed, was downcast, when I should have been smiling and joyful at the promise of marriage to a successful businessman like Simon. I knew him well, but it took me by surprise. It was not for me to answer.

Lazarus and Martha looked at me with pleasant smiles on their faces. Uncle Elias beamed with pride. "Her brother Lazarus and I will promise Mary, who is sometimes willful, to you as your wife. You have offered silver and two lambs for the bride price. She is priceless, but I accept the gifts for her."

We all sipped wine in agreement. "Shalom. To life and to health."

I finally found my tongue. "I am honored to have such a fine proposal, but I had hoped to devote my life to serving the community of Jesus's followers. Now I suppose that is up to Simon."

"I am beholden to Jesus as he healed me. I believe I was made well for a reason and not only to give a small gift to the Temple. Mary, I am happy to hear you also want to serve and proclaim the good news of Jesus's death and resurrection. When I travel afar to conduct business, I would like for you to come with me to tell people about Jesus and what he has done for us all."

"It would please me very much to go with you and tell people about Jesus. I cannot think of anything I would rather do." Marriage had not been on my mind at all, and while it was a surprise, I could not refuse so kind an offer.

Martha was still smiling. I turned to her, "I need to ask your forgiveness for marrying before you do."

She shook her head, smiling. "You already know I was espoused first, and when he died I chose to do diaconate work instead of accepting another to marry. You do not need to ask for forgiveness, but you do have it with my love, little sister."

As I thought about my younger self, I recalled what a willful girl I had been then. How blessed I am to live to see the day I would wed a good man.

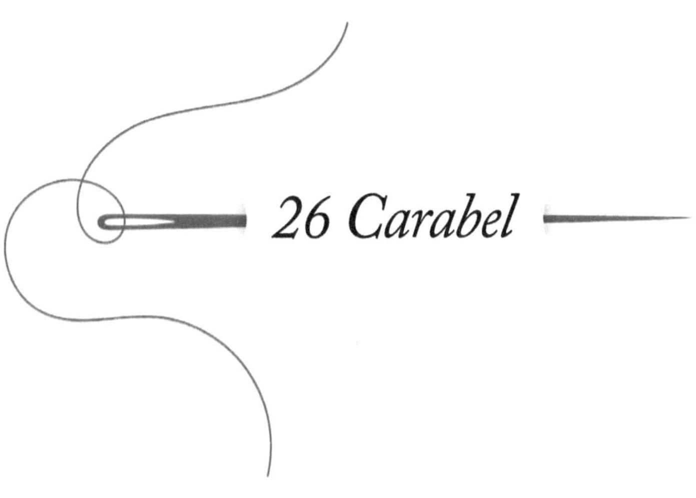

26 Carabel

"A friend loves at all times."

Proverbs 17:17a

I screamed and shook in terror when the men abducted me and left my herd of sheep stranded on the rocky hillside. It had already been a dreadful day to begin as my father had raised his voice at me for staying too long abed. He wanted to sleep after shepherding all night and having spent several days looking for a good place for our sheep to forage for food. He had scolded me and threatened to beat me if I did not hurry out. He had never laid a hand on me, but I knew he was more bereft after my mother died.

I heard the donkey cart before I saw them, but was not concerned. I lifted my hand to wave. It was probably some men with goods in a cart to sell or bringing something home.

Taken by surprise, I had no time to react when they grabbed me, except to scream. No one was near enough to hear besides the young woman tied up inside the cart where they threw me in.

She let out a groan of pain as I landed on her. We settled as best we could packed like sheaves taken to market. Mary became my companion and sometimes savior during our ordeal in the cart and then our trip in the boat. She was a lively girl and she had faith. I had no faith in a benevolent God. She assured me we would be rescued. I could not summon the same thoughts and was ever thankful to her for being with me. We became so aware of each other, we thwarted one sailor's attempt to bring one of us below deck for evil purposes. We had acted as a team with signals rather than words and had knocked the man on his back by our efforts.

I did not miss my sheep except for the little wooly lambs. I was homesick for them. It was not something to be concerned about as I had no control over my life. I feared we would be standing in a slave market, poked and prodded by buyers. It was a quiet purchase agreement. When we were bought to be concubines by a man who owned a large home in the desert, I slept in the softest bed I had ever had and ate more costly food as well. I had no other work to do, as my room was cleaned and clothes provided which I did not have to clean or mend. It was a good place to be.

The Master Arthrimian was a kind man who did not hurry me. He had a woman come to show and tell me things I needed to know about how to please him before I spent one night in his chambers. It went well. I was caressed by him and complimented for my beauty. I had never thought of myself as beautiful before. He reclined at a low table with me to partake of rich-tasting meat, fresh vegetables, exotic fruit, and fine bread. He raised a cup of wine to my lips, and said, "Here is a sweet wine to ease you, my dear, beautiful Cara. Sip and enjoy. Soon we will taste and find pleasure in each other."

In the midst of my getting used to a very different life, I became charmed and thought little about my companion, Mary. She was not wise in the ways of the world and had told me about how much she had relied on her brother and sister. Her parents had died a few years earlier and she missed her mother. She often talked of Martha as being bossy, but I could see the pride she had in the way her sister conducted herself. I would have liked to meet her brother Lazarus, as she spoke in glowing terms about him and his friends.

I had especially grown close to her during the time on the ship as the slavers sent us to the man who had bought us. We had thwarted a deckhand who wanted to have us for himself even though it was forbidden. We were goods to be delivered intact. Neither of us saw him afterwards, so we believed his actions had earned him time in chains out of our sight.

After a few days at Master Arthrimian's house, I realized I had not seen Mary walking in the hallway, or at a meal. I inquired of Ulta if she was ill. He said he did not want to tell me. When I would not stop asking, he said Sangee had told him Mary had tried to escape. Sangee was very upset as he told him when someone was sent to look for her, they found she had been taken by a wild animal and only her tunic stained with blood was found. I wept, thinking of my friend Mary dying in such a terrible way. She had such a strong faith she would be rescued. I was remorseful at not asking to see her again to speak with her once we were both settled in the house of Arthrimian.

There is much more to my life as Master Arthrimian's concubine. He favored me, and I was moved to chambers next to his, even more luxurious than I had before. Time passed and he did not marry a wife as I had been told he had planned. One day he asked me to accompany him to Cairo. I saw the lovely carriage he had to take us there. He would do business, and I would be driven around Cairo to see all the sights. I was a little disquieted as I could not forget how I had been abducted before I had ended here in such luxury. I decided to be vigilant, and not let myself be overcome by some assailant.

As I was being taken through the streets of Cairo, I was met with a most excellent surprise.

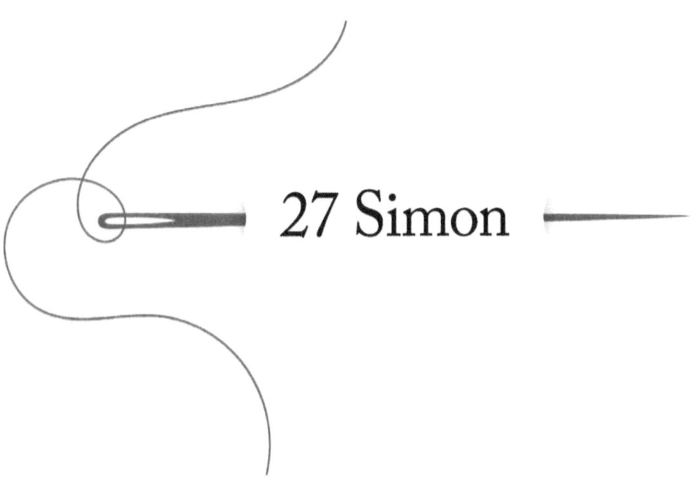

27 Simon

I am my beloved's and his desire is for me.

Song of Songs 7:10

One year later, Mary and I were married in the courtyard by our homes. It was a wonderful celebration with friends and neighbors attending. We ate delicious food, drank wine and danced. Martha insisted on hosting. Ott and Naomi, with hired servants from Jerusalem, did much of the preparation.

Joy prevailed for a week of celebration. We men danced in a circle. Soon Martha, Mary of Magdala, Joanna, and many women joined hands and welcomed Mary into their circle as they danced the hora to the beat of little drums and tambourines by a group from Jerusalem. Mary was a happy bride. I never stopped smiling.

It is a companionable marriage, agreeable to us, and Mary is a precious wife. Ott and Naomi remained on as our servants.

Mary told me she used to wish to travel to places she had never seen but was reluctant because of the bad memories of abduction. I enticed her with descriptions of exotic places. She agreed to go to Egypt with me on a business trip. While she had been there captive, she had not seen any of the wonders. She described her time as only fear, danger, despair, and endless sand. Now I could protect her so she could see the wondrous sights. We came to Ethiopia, where we found a fellowship of people who called their god Adonai, and who believed Jesus the promised Messiah had come. A few new synagogues were being built.

I spoke with a man who told of stonecutters who had been digging in the rock of the earth to create a place of worship. It would take a long time for them to finish even one, but the structure had slowly begun to take shape in the bowels of the earth. I could not persuade one of the stonecutters to come back to Jerusalem and create tombs, because he thought the project of making a building inside the earth would be more of a challenge. I shook my head, wondering if it was even possible to create such a meeting place for Followers of the Way. As it turned out, it took a long time for the underground synagogues to be fully completed. I never saw the area again.

Egypt in all its glory was truly magnificent, with large stone statuary everywhere. Mary was awed as she had seen none of it when she was there as a slave captive. Most people there did not worship YHWH, the God of Abraham, but paid homage to pharaohs, the sun god, and other stone-figured gods. There were very rich people in the city of Cairo where I transacted business with stone artisans and merchandise traders.

I knew Esa and and his wife Pompeo, who were guides who knew the area well. I asked them to show Mary the wonders of the area. I told them about Jesus and was delighted they were already believers. I left to do business and later Mary told me about her day.

She said, "As we were strolling the stone street, I saw a carriage coming toward us with a lovely sunshade of many colors atop. Upon coming nearer, the carriage pulled by black horses slowed. Sitting on red padded seats, and almost unrecognizable, was Carabel. Her face was more rounded and fair with rose-colored lips and cheeks, and kohl swept markings on her eyelids. Lavish jewels at her neck and ears flashed in the sunlight. I was almost afraid to make myself known, because I had stolen away from our Master Arthrimian, but I blurted out her name."

My wife became more excited as she continued. "The carriage stopped. Carabel leaned forward to look at me but made no attempt to leave her fine perch. 'Who is it who knows my name?'"

"I asked her if she recognized me, whether she was doing well and if she was still with Master Arthrimian. Shock sparked in her widened eyes, and her lovely mouth gaped open. She said she could not believe she was seeing me alive because after I had fled, they told her I was dead. One of the servants had said I had tried to escape and was destroyed by a wild animal. No one could tell her what happened. She told me that my old servant Sangie had been distraught. Carabel is still with the master and treated very well. She's Arthrimian's favorite consort and said is better than herding sheep as she did before she was captured. He allows her to come with him to visit Cairo sometimes as she was today."

"I told her I was blessed I saw her doing well. I told her how I escaped and traveled back to my home. I told her I was married to a businessman, whom I accompanied here. When I professed I was kept safe by YHWH and his son, Jesus, when I escaped, she said she had never heard of the Judean God having a son."

I was thrilled to have Mary so lively telling me about seeing the other girl who had been captured by slavers.

She was not anxious or fearful as I had thought she would be with a reminder of an awful time in her life. It had given her the opportunity to teach Carabel about Jesus.

She told Carabel, "Jesus was the promised Messiah we heard about when we were growing up. He came, he loved, he healed people, taught the truth, and finally vexed the authorities so much that they arrested and convicted him, and nailed him to a cross to crucify him. But it was not the last word. Jesus rose from the dead and ascended to his Father in Heaven where he lives for us today."

Carabel had answered her, "Rose from his death? You give me a lot to think about. I am happy as I am in my position as the favored woman. Master Arthrimian has not married, so it is as if I am his wife. I have many privileges."

Mary told me she watched Carabel's carriage roll away and knew she had made the right choice not to ask her to escape with her. Her captive companion was happy.

With business taken care of, I was ready to return home. We stopped many places along the way where we both proclaimed the gospel of Jesus and were invited to stay in homes where there were believers. Sometimes there was a language difference, but usually, someone interpreted. Our common belief in Jesus was the key to our understanding one another.

It became our way of life. I told everyone about my miraculous healing from leprosy, and about Lazarus being raised by Jesus. The best news we had to share in every place we went was that Jesus died and was raised on the third day. He is with his Father YHWH in heaven where he has prepared a place for all who believe in him and follow him.

Jesus's disciples were filled with the Holy Spirit and went to many countries preaching the wonderful news of his redeeming love. Jesus had asked them to go and tell people about him and his ministry of love. Many had faith to bring healing and some to restore life to people.

Some people rejected us and would not invite us to return after they heard what we had to say. One such time, we were greeted by a fine family who had made a nourishing meal for us. When I began to tell them about my healing from being a leper, one woman moved away from the table. When I proclaimed Jesus's death and resurrection, the man cleared his throat loudly. After the meal was finished, we were not asked to stay as was customary.

I felt very discouraged as we trudged down the street looking for a place to lay our heads for the night. "The Lord will provide. After all, I spent many a night beneath a gnarled old tree when I had leprosy," I said.

Mary smiled. "You are right. I found many places to rest as I was making my way back to Bethany."

We spread our cloaks and slept on the ground while the starry sky kept watch.

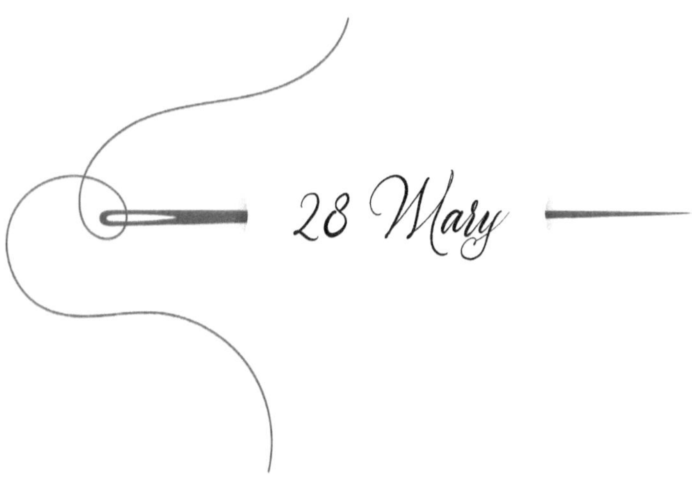

28 Mary

Those who wait for the Lord shall renew their strength, they shall mount up with wings like eagles, they shall run and not be weary, they shall walk and not faint.

Isaiah 40:31

I bore Simon a son we named Joshua a year after our marriage. Ott and his family became believers in the resurrected Jesus. They played with our little boy and gave me time to rest. Martha still did her diaconate work but found time to help me tend to her beloved nephew. She enjoyed playing with Joshua. Uncle Elias became of great age and could not hear well, but his sight was strong enough to see Joshua. He loved to dandle him on his knee and chant songs.

Simon was overjoyed we had a son. It was a good life. He recalled how he had to have enough faith for Jesus to heal him, and he was forever grateful for being cured of his leprosy. He told anyone who would listen about Jesus, the Savior of the world, but he often confessed to me, "While I am not the self-centered businessman I was before I got leprosy and was healed, I often wonder if I now am conducting my life as wisely and faith-filled as I should. My speech is not eloquent words, and sometimes I think I am not doing enough. I tend to talk about business and political issues instead of Jesus."

"You are a wonderful man, and I am grateful for YHWH bringing us together. I have grown in faith as well as learned to conduct myself as a wife and mother. We have a loving family, and I am satisfied. I believe it is enough."

"I know you will not travel with me while Joshua is suckling, but I must go attend to business far away. I trust you and Joshua will be safe here with your sister and brother living nearby.

"Please be careful. I will be very well here as I have my family and have become fast friends with Ott and Naomi." I had a secret as I believed my womb had been opened once again and I would bear another child. Simon and I were truly blessed. Yet with him going far away, I worried about his safety as we lived with political unrest.

He was going to the port city of Caesarea Maritima. Roman government under the rule of Herod Antipas maintained military headquarters there. Roman Troops had been moved from Jerusalem to there as well. I trusted YHWH, but I fretted lest some volatile sentry not like the looks of him and cast him into prison or kill him on sight.

29 Simon

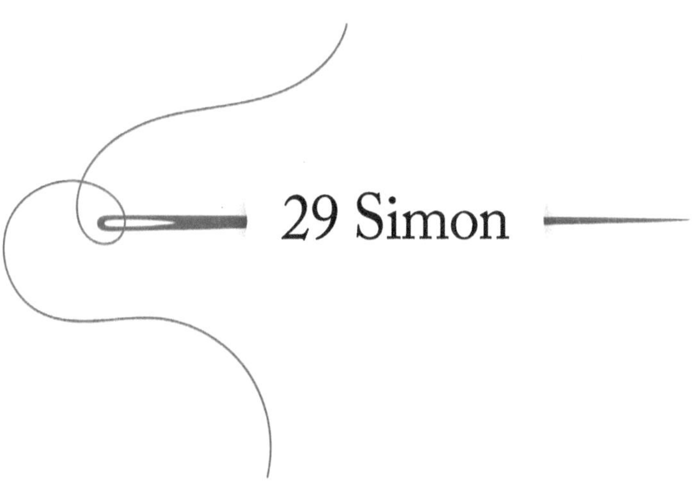

You shall love the Lord your God with all your heart, and all your soul, and with all your might. Keep these words that I am commanding you today in your heart. Recite them to your children and talk about them when you are at home, and when you are away, when you lie down and when you rise.

Deuteronomy 6:4

Mary stayed in Bethany with our Joshua when I left. My hired carriage stopped in Caesarea Maritima where I was to catch a boat going to Rome. It was a bustling port with a large military presence. I felt intimidated by the Roman soldiers, even more than I ever had in Jerusalem. A troop marched in even ranks down the main street and stopped as if halted by an unseen hand, all saluted by pounding their chest once in unison when a superior officer approached.

I kept to the side, minding my own business. One soldier, eyeing my Judean garments, stopped me. "What business have you here?"

I paused before I answered. I knew John the Baptist had displeased Herod Antipas. Perhaps they thought I was one of his followers. "I have business in Rome and seek passage to go there to transact trade arrangements." I carried a satchel of business information inked on papyrus. Besides business, I had a small papyrus roll of stories relating to Jesus.

He lowered his sword but kept it unsheathed and waved me on without a word. I hurried to find the small ship which would take me to Rome. But when I got to the port, no ship waited. I could not believe I had arrived late. I did not know what happened, or what my next step should be. Thankfully, Mary and my son were not with me if there was any trouble.

I asked a dock worker if he knew what had happened. "The only ship in port, other than the big grain ship we are unloading, sailed about an hour ago.

This one is scheduled to remain in port until repairs are done."

I thanked him and wandered around thinking about the problem I was facing. There were always delays, but I hoped it would not be too long before I could go. Young boys were playing some game where each of them had a stick and were lobbing a makeshift ball of rags tied in string. They were laughing and yelling in such a carefree way. I smiled, despite my dilemma.

As I was distracted, I did not see the Roman soldier until I heard his hobnailed soles clicking on the stone walkway behind me. I turned abruptly, ready to grasp my knife from its sheath at my side. He had his gladius unsheathed and his face was an unreadable scowl.

"Come with me." He motioned with the gladius.

I nodded, and followed him, not at all sure what he wanted. We walked on uneven stones and turned from the busy port area to a street where stone and brick homes stood in a row. No trees, flowers, or baskets decorated the fronts. I heard little children squealing somewhere, no doubt in the courtyards behind the houses. I could smell spicy cooking aromas. We made a right turn into another street, and yet another until we came to a building I presumed to be his headquarters. We mounted the steps, and he met an officer with a shining helmet. He immediately saluted him with a right fist bump to his own chest.

I was led to a room where a man who wore a purple striped toga sat on a soft red-covered bench. He waved me to a stone bench and dismissed the officer without a word. The officer nodded, saluted, and backed out of the room before closing the door.

I decided silence was my best defense until I knew why I had been summoned. The unsmiling older man, eyed me thoughtfully before he spoke. "I suppose you are wondering why you have been brought to my chambers."

"Yes." Sweat began to form on my forehead.

"Are you a Follower of the Way?" He gave the slightest hint of a smile beneath a short-clipped mustache, and he used a soft white hand to put a strand of grey hair behind his ear.

"I am." I would not lie. Now the back of my neck itched and made me recoil as it reminded me of my years as a scorned leper. I wondered if I now would be put in chains and imprisoned for my new faith. I wondered if Jesus knew how doing what he had asked imperiled his friends. Could I handle it?

He eyed me silently for a time, then clapped his hands twice. A young woman slave in a plain tunic came quickly and knelt in front of him. He motioned for her to stand. "Bring us the day wine, some cheese, and fresh bread. Get this man a basin of water and cloths to wash his hands, and bring Babar with water and towels to bathe his feet."

When all the washing had been done, the man ordered the door closed and bolted. I wondered if it was for our safety or only his.

He invited me to recline on the couch beside a low table where the meal and wine had been placed. He bowed his head and closed his eyes. I wondered if he was thanking the Roman gods for the blessings. He raised his wine cup and nodded. I raised mine as well. I could contain myself no longer. "What do you intend to do to me? You arrested me and asked me if I followed Jesus. Now you are giving me food and drink, for which I am grateful. I do not even know your name or what your position is in Caesarea Maritima. I am a business merchant, Simon of Bethany, a former leper, healed by Jesus. Please—"

"You may call me Leonitis. I am a judge as well as a member of the High Council." He lowered his voice to a whisper. "I am also a new Follower of the Way. Even my family does not know, and the soldier who brought you in is one of the followers." When he saw you wandering the streets and recognized you as a Judean, he thought I might like to talk with you. He knew nothing about you, save the calm demeanor one does not normally see on the face of a businessman who has not caught his ship as he had hoped."

"I thank you, Leonitis. I am hungry and eager to speak with you. I am not sure where I will stay until another ship is ready to depart."

He clapped his hands and the young woman hurried in and knelt at his feet. "Rise, child. See if there is a room at the inn nearest the port where my guest can stay until the next ship departs."

We conversed, and I told him about how I had endured leprosy and been healed by Jesus. He told me how the missionary Paul had come and been arrested and put in prison but was set free. He met Paul, who survived under dire circumstances. Leonitis had come to believe what Paul told him about the eternal life Jesus created for all with his death and resurrection. I would have much to tell Mary when I arrived home. My stay at the Port Inn was comfortable enough, even with a lumpy sleeping mattress. The food was alright, but some rich, hot Roman spiced sauces were not to my liking. In spite of everything, I could tell YHWH had put me there as the buyer for the cook at the Port Inn ordered some exotic spices for which Leonitis was willing to pay a handsome price.

I was able to sail the next day. My trip on the water was uneventful save a short argument among the crew which caused one of them to be so injured he hobbled around doing his deck work. My heart was still soaring with the joy of the unusual "arrest" in Caesarea Maritima where I had met a fellow Jesus believer. I also had a new business contract with the buyer at the Port Inn. YHWH was with me, and I could do anything. Or could I?

Once my business was taken care of in Rome, I sought other of my countrymen who now lived there. The missionary named Paul was speaking there. He had been named Saul before his conversion by Christ and had previously been responsible for persecuting

Jesus's Followers of the Way." Paul had been called by a revelation of Jesus to be one to spread the gospel. I listened, fascinated by his elocution, his wisdom. In one such meeting, people asked many questions.

Paul had been a Pharisee, and was still a Pharisee in name, but not participating as others did in Jerusalem. I stayed to learn from him but came away from his lectures more confused about what I should be doing than I had before I went.

Paul invited me to the house where he was staying with friends who made tents. People were enjoying a simple meal of bread and wine. We lounged at a table in the Roman way. People were laughing and visiting. I asked, "How can I serve the risen Lord? I am only good at business transactions. I do not have a way with preaching words as you do."

Paul took a big swallow of wine and wiped his mouth with his sleeve. He clapped me on the shoulder, and said, "You have a beautiful wife and son and a thriving honest business. Therein is your service. Not all men can preach and teach in the same way, but each of us must serve as YHWH and his son Jesus call and give us the talent, strength, and courage. We are all granted salvation through grace, not only by works. Be honest in business and go home to your family. The family is the foundation of all which is to come. You teach children and all you meet by your everyday words and actions to love and serve the risen Jesus."

With Paul's words resounding in my head, I traveled

home to my wonderful wife Mary and son in Bethany, and praised our Lord every day for his gracious physical and spiritual healing of me and so many others.

With my arms wide open to embrace my Mary, I came into the house to hear the babbling, "Papa" greeting of Joshua.

When we were alone enjoying wine in the evening, I said, "I missed my ship, and while I was waiting for another I was arrested and brought before a judge in Caesarea Maritima."

"How terrible for you!" She clung to my hand.

"I'm sorry I upset you. It seemed like a real arrest, but the man only wanted to privately meet another Follower of the Way, as even his own family do not know. It would be dangerous for him as he is a judge. He feared they would ship him off to Rome to face the lions. He also helped me secure a room at the Port Inn. While there I talked with a man who gave me an order to supply them with spices. YHWH smiles on us."

Mary became quiet and had tears in her eyes. "What is wrong, my dearest?" I asked.

"I did not tell you about our expecting another child before you left, because I wanted to surprise you. Sadly, my womb emptied before its time, and Martha and I buried what would have been our second child while you were away."

I let her cry, feeling remorse at being gone, held her, and stroked her hair. "I am sorry I was not here for you. Our God will bless us when He chooses. You are so brave to bear these trials alone while I am away on business."

She nestled her head on my chest, and I cradled her in my arms.

"I wish you would never have to leave."

I tried to think of the right thing to say to my wife, but words failed me. Having a business was my way to provide for my family. I didn't know another trade.

The next time I scheduled travel for business, Mary asked to come along and bring Joshua. She mended my ragged feelings and my torn garments, and we were whole. We served the Lord as best we could. As YHWH had ordained, we were one in body, mind, and spirit.

Glossary

Ankh – An ancient Egyptian symbol of life. It is a cross with a loop at the top.

Bar mitzvah – A Jewish boy who has reached his thirteenth birthday and reached the age of religious duty. It is the ceremony to recognize the boy's coming of age.

Beelzebul – An evil being, the devil.

Diaconate –A board of deacons or deaconesses who serve the followers of Christ. Martha was a woman who served by providing meals and sewing or mending.

El – Elohim, an ancient name for God.

Festival of Weeks – A festival to celebrate the first fruits of the harvest.

Furlong – One-eighth of a mile.

Gladius – Sword.

Hora – A folk dance of Israel in which dancers form a circle, lock arms, and dance to the left or right with grapevine steps and hops.

Leprosy – An infectious disease that attacks skin, tissues, and nerves. It is characterized by nodules, ulcers, and white scaly scabs, deformities, and wasting of body parts.

Leptons – Small coins worth less than a penny.

Mikveh – *Mikva*. A ritual cleansing bath, usually with seven steps.

Ossuary – A stone box used to store bones inside ancient tombs.

Passover – A holiday celebrating the time when the angel of death passed over all the Jewish families, but slew non-Jew's children in Egypt when Pharaoh refused to allow enslaved Jews to go back to their homeland.

Paul – (Saul) A prominent Pharisee who had persecuted the followers of Jesus. In a very dramatic encounter, Jesus met him, changed his name to Paul, and commissioned him to stop what he was doing and preach the gospel.

Pharisee – A member of the Jewish sect who rigidly adhered to ancient written and oral laws.

Ra – Egyptian sun god, depicted as having the head of a hawk and wearing a solar disk as a crown.

Rabbi – Teacher.

Sadducees – A member of a Jewish sect at the time of Jesus who denied the existence of angels and did not believe in the resurrection of the dead. They opposed the Pharisees point of view.

Shiva – After the burial of a loved one, the family and close friends sat together for seven days mourning out of respect.

Shofar – A ram's horn used as a trumpet for various religious services. A ram's horn is used to commemorate the sacrifice of Isaac being stopped by a ram for Abraham to sacrifice instead of his son.

Steles – Posts that contain inscriptions.

Talit – A shawl or covering, sometimes fringed, worn by those who were going to prayer time.

Torn – In deep grief, family and close friends tore their garments to express mourning.

Tefillin – Phylacteries often tied on the hands and arms. "And though shalt bind them for a sign upon thy hand." Deuteronomy 6:8.

YHWH – Yahweh, the Jewish name for the Lord, their God, whose name they could not utter.

About The Author

E. Ruth Harder

The author grew up on a farm in Uvalde County Texas. She married Charles Harder (deceased, 2003) in 1957. She was a Technical Information Specialist at Lawrence Livermore National Laboratory until retirement. She achieved a Masters in Library Science from San Jose State University in San Jose, California. She says, "Critique groups and workshops of the California Writers Club Tri-Valley Branch help keep me motivated as I pursue my passion for writing."

Advances in Library Administration and Organization, Vol. 13, 1995, published her work, "Library Automation's Effect on the Interior Design of California Public Libraries." Her poem "Widow's Window," was published in the *2014 California Writers Club Tri-Valley Branch anthology, Encore.* "A Light in Every Corner" is in the *2014 Word Movers, An Anthology of Creative Writings by Seniors.*

Novels, *Hannah Weaver of Life,* (2015), *The Unbroken Thread,* (2020), Russian Hill Press.

"Daily prayer and Bible studies and my Holy Cross Lutheran Church family and those at Faith Lutheran in Kamiah, Idaho, both keep me focused on what is most important in my life — the eternal blessings of our Lord and Savior, Jesus Christ."

www.ingramcontent.com/pod-product-compliance
Lightning Source LLC
Chambersburg PA
CBHW020753310726
48969CB00002B/515